Cinders and Sparks

FAIRIES IN THE FOREST

Also by Lindsey Kelk

Magic at Midnight

Cinders and Sparks

FAIRIES IN THE FOREST

LINDSEY KELK

Illustrated by Pippa Curnick

HARPER
An Imprint of HarperCollins*Publishers*

Cinders and Sparks #2: Fairies in the Forest

For information address HarperCollins Children's Books, a division of HarperCollins Publishers, 195 Broadway, New York, NY 10007.
www.harpercollinschildrens.com
ISBN 978-0-06-300671-3
Typography by Corina Lupp
21 22 23 24 25 BRR 10 9 8 7 6 5 4 3 2 1
❖
First published in Great Britain in 2019 by HarperCollins Children's Books, a division of HarperCollins Publishers Ltd.
First US Edition, 2021

For Penelope Rose Nancy Clay

May all your wishes come true

and may you never have to do the dishes

Chapter One

"HANSEL!" CINDERS SQUEALED. "IF you don't loosen your grip, you're going to be walking the rest of the way to Fairyland."

"Perhaps you ought to let me be in front for a while," Hansel replied, slackening his arms just a little. "I'm very strong and I wouldn't mind if you needed to hold on to me to feel safe."

"You're going to need more than something to hold on to to feel safe in a minute,"

Cinders muttered back. "My horse, my quest, my rules."

Cinders was on a very important mission to find out some *very* important things, and it was bad enough having to listen to Sparks, her magical talking dog, rattle on about sausages, or lack thereof, without a boy in a silly hat giving her grief. Every time Mouse the horse (Mouse was a mouse who Cinders had accidentally turned into a horse, but that was another story altogether) took a sharp turn to avoid running into a tree or off the edge of a cliff, Hansel would let out a terrible shriek and squeeze Cinders's waist so tight she thought she might snap in two.

"Perhaps you shouldn't have invited him along in the first place," Sparks suggested from his comfortable position curled up in front of

Cinders, his muzzle resting in Mouse's mane.

"Excuse me, you were the one who said he should come along when he offered you those sausages," Cinders reminded him. "Honestly, Sparks, I don't think there's anything you wouldn't do for a sausage."

Sparks considered this for a moment, decided there was a good chance that she might be right, and so said nothing.

It felt as though they'd been riding for days, but really it had only been a few hours since Cinders had escaped King Picklebottom's guards and fled the palace. But, as they rode deeper into the forest and the air grew chilly, she was starting to wonder if they'd made the right decision. Long, spindly branches wove themselves together overhead, blocking out the sun, and the farther they went, the darker and darker and darker the sky became until Cinders could barely see her hand in front of her face.

Thankfully, she was very, very brave. Most of the time. She wasn't afraid of anything—King Picklebottom, the Dark Forest, munklepoops, gadzoozles, or nobbledizooks. Not that she'd ever been in the Dark Forest before or met a munklepoop, gadzoozle, or nobbledizook in real life. All she knew was that she had to get to Fairyland. Just a week ago, she'd been living in the countryside with her father and her stepsisters and her really rather awful stepmother. An ordinary girl with an ordinary life. And then one day, out of nowhere, her fairy godmother had arrived and Cinders had started to develop magic powers, and everything had changed.

"Cinders." Hansel ducked his head to avoid getting slapped in the chops by a low-hanging branch. "Can I ask you a question?"

"Yes, Hansel."

"You said your mom was a fairy?"

"Yes, Hansel."

"Which means you're half fairy?"

"Yes, Hansel."

"So why don't you cast a spell and magic us all to Fairyland rather than riding through the Dark Forest?"

Cinders sighed. If they'd been through this once, they'd been through it a thousand times.

"Because my magic isn't strong enough," she said as she flicked Mouse's reins, encouraging him to go just a little bit faster. "I only found out I was half fairy a week ago. These things don't work themselves out overnight, you know. I mean, if I'd been more in control of my powers, I wouldn't have made that pig come back to life at dinner, I wouldn't have scared the king, he wouldn't have decided I was a witch, and we wouldn't have had to run away in the first place."

Cinders couldn't help but wonder if it wouldn't have been easier to just stay at the palace, marry Prince Joderick, and behave herself. Except she didn't want to marry Prince Joderick, and she never had been very good at behaving herself. But now she was lost in the forest with the palace guards after her, and the only thing she could think to do was go to Fairyland, where her mother apparently came from, and try to get some answers.

"Fair enough, fair enough," said Hansel.

He closed his eyes as Mouse leaped over a fallen tree trunk and thundered on, deeper into the forest.

"One more question. Do you think your magic might be strong enough to find us a toilet? I really have to go."

Truly, she should have left that boy where she'd found him.

"It's not my fault!" he wailed when she spurred Mouse on to ride faster. "It's all this jiggling around on the back of the horse. I drank a massive bottle of elderberry juice this morning and I've been holding it in for ages."

"Can't you wait ten more minutes?" she asked.

"Not unless you want an accident," he grumbled, "and I don't think that's a good idea on the back of a horse."

All Cinders wanted to do was keep riding, avoid being eaten by a munklepoop, get to Fairyland, and solve the mystery of how her mother had found her way into the kingdom, met her dad, given birth to Cinders, and left her with a magical talking dog. Was that really too much to ask for?

"All right, all right, we'll stop." Cinders closed her eyes, concentrated very hard and took a deep breath. "I wish we could find somewhere for Sparks to eat some sausages, Mouse to get some cheese, and Hansel to have a pee because he's a useless boy who can't even hold it in for a minute."

"Oh, really," Sparks sniffed, turning up his shiny black nose. "There's no need to be vulgar."

All at once, Cinders felt a tingling in her fingertips. As they reached the darkest part of the Dark Forest, her hands began to glow silver and gold, thousands of tiny lights flickering brightly all around her.

"Oh, I say!" Hansel grabbed hold of his green felt hat. "What's she doing?"

"What do you mean *what's she doing*?" Sparks asked a little indignantly. "She's using her magic to find you a bathroom, just like you asked!"

Hansel looked shocked, the rosy-red color disappearing from his round cheeks.

"So she really *is* half fairy?"

"Not everyone is a fibber," replied Sparks.

Hansel went very quiet. He had a reputation as a world-class porky-pie teller and not without good reason.

"Look!" The light from Cinders's hands suddenly began to flow outward, carving a golden path through the pitch-black of the forest floor. "I think we're supposed to go this way."

"Follow me!" Sparks cried bravely, hopping down from Mouse's saddle to race ahead of his friends.

"So you can smell the sausages, as well?" Cinders asked.

"Certainly can," he confirmed. "Top-notch wishing, Cinders. Very well done."

Chapter Two

A FEW MINUTES LATER, THE golden path faded away and the foursome found themselves in a little clearing. Cinders looked up and saw stars in the night sky. It was much later than she'd realized. In the middle of the clearing was a sweet little cottage. The walls were white and the roof was thatched, and there was an archway of roses growing around the wooden front door.

“Really, very well done, Cinders,” Sparks said as he bounded up to the cottage, marveling at the perfectly tended little garden full of pretty flowers. *All the better to pee on later*, he thought to himself.

“Let’s see if anyone is home,” Cinders said, straightening her shoulders and trying to tidy her messy hair. She held up her non-sparkly

hand and knocked on the door. No one answered.

"Knock again," Hansel suggested, crossing his legs and doing a little dance from side to side. "Louder this time. They probably couldn't hear it."

"Perhaps they're in the kitchen cooking," Sparks agreed with his eyes closed. Something inside smelled very good indeed.

And so Cinders knocked again, but there was still no answer.

"Try the door," Sparks suggested, popping his paws up on the windowsill and peeking in.

Cinders gave a cross little sigh. She really, really, really wanted to get on with her journey.

"Honestly, Sparks, nice people don't go around leaving their front doors unlocked for just anyone to walk in and—"

The handle turned in her hand, the door opened, and Hansel raced past her and disappeared down the hallway.

"Hello?" Cinders called. "Is anyone home?"

She turned on a lamp to get a better look at the place, which appeared to be empty. In the living room there was a fireplace, and in front of it was one big chair, one medium-sized chair, and one little chair. Walking into the kitchen, she saw a large wooden table. Placed around it was one big chair, one medium-sized chair, and one little chair.

"Would you look at that!" Sparks bounded up onto the smallest chair, walked around in a circle, and plopped his red, fluffy tail down on the comfy cushion. "Perfectly Sparks-sized."

Still not altogether sure about being in someone else's house uninvited, Cinders tapped an uncertain finger on the arm of the

biggest chair. It was awfully late, and she was awfully tired. It had been a peculiar day to say the least. She was only having a sit-down, after all. Surely no one would mind?

"Good golly gosh, that's a comfy chair," she gasped as she sank into the cushion. She could have closed her eyes and gone to sleep right there and then.

"Cinders! Sparks!"

Quick as a flash, Cinders and her doggy pal ran off to find out what was wrong with Hansel.

"Hansel! Even I know you shouldn't wear your shoes in bed!"

The bothersome boy was in the bedroom, in a great big bed with the covers tucked up to his chin.

"It's so soft," he said, plucking off his hat

and placing it on the bedside table. "And look, there's one for each of us! It's as if they knew we were coming."

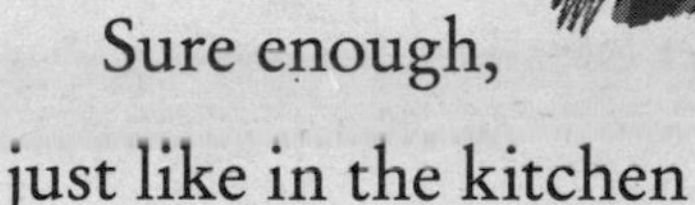

Sure enough, just like in the kitchen and the living room, the bedroom had one big bed, one medium-sized bed, and one little bed. And Cinders was awfully tired . . .

"I hate to agree with Hansel, but I think he's got the right idea here," Sparks said, making himself comfortable in the smallest bed. "We'll sleep here tonight and start out for Fairyland in the morning. No point trotting off through the forest half asleep, is there?"

"What about the people who own this house?" Cinders asked, gazing at the medium-sized bed with its big fat pillows and fluffy white blankets.

"We'll leave them a nice note," Sparks declared.

"Everyone loves getting a nice note," Hansel said, already dozing. "Come on, Cinders. Who would send us back out into the forest in the middle of the night?"

"Well, King Picklebottom for one," she replied. "My stepmother for another. And all the people you've managed to annoy in the village, including your own sister."

"All very good points we should discuss in the morning," Hansel muttered sleepily, rolling over and turning out the light. "Good-night, Cinders."

A tap at the window made her jump, but it was only Mouse, keen to find out what was happening inside.

"I think you should get comfortable," Cinders said, opening the window and giving him a scratch between his rather large ears. "Looks like we're staying here for the night."

Mouse squeaked happily and curled up underneath the low cottage window.

Cinders climbed into the middle bed, Hansel and Sparks already snoring on either side of her. Maybe a couple hours of rest was a good idea, and then they could start out fresh first thing in the morning.

"Just one day away from Fairyland," she muttered as she closed her eyes. "And finding out who my mother really was."

Chapter Three

BACK IN CINDERS'S LITTLE pink cottage in the woods, no one was sleeping.

"I'm very sorry," Cinders's dad said, scratching his head, "but could you run that past me again?"

Prince Joderick Jorenson Picklebottom took a deep breath and started to tell his story for the third time. "Basically, the part you really need to know is that my father, the king, has declared

Cinders a witch and exiled her forever."

Margery, Cinders's stepmother, held one hand to her forehead and swooned, collapsing onto a conveniently placed couch behind her.

"A witch!" she declared as her two daughters, Agnes and Eleanor, rushed to her side. "I always knew there was something up with that girl."

"But Cinders couldn't possibly be a witch!" said Cinders's father, looking distraught.

Meanwhile, Joderick was eyeing a plate of tasty-looking cookies on the kitchen table. He really had ridden quite a long way, and he would have loved a quick snack before he rode back to the palace. But with all the crying and swooning, this didn't really seem like the time to help himself.

"If Prince Joderick says she's a witch, she's a witch," Margery declared. "I know she's your daughter, but I think she's had you under some sort of spell. We always knew she was shifty, didn't we, girls?"

"Oh, yes," Elly replied at once.

"Did we?" Aggy asked.

"I didn't say she *is* a witch," Joderick said, inching closer to the cookies. *Hmm, were those raisins or chocolate chips?* "I said my dad *thinks* she's a witch."

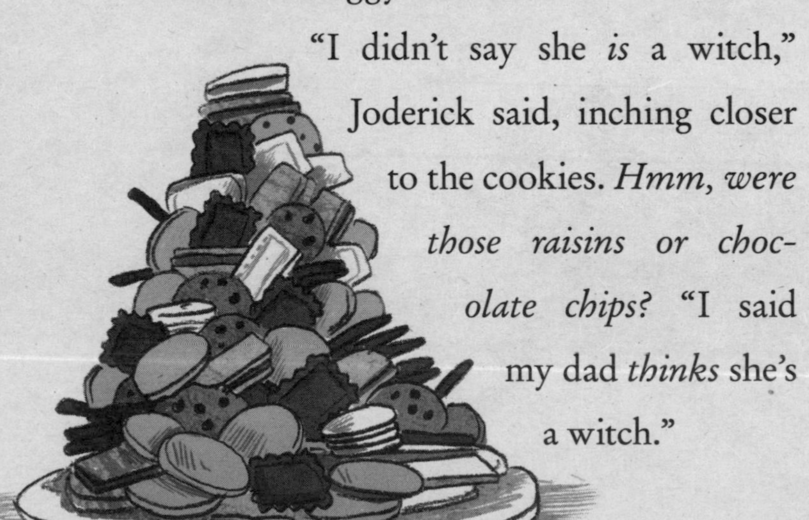

Cinders's stepmother fixed Joderick with an unpleasant smile. "But if she isn't a witch, why would he think that she was?"

"Um . . . there was some unpleasantness at dinner," he muttered. "Involving some magic and a roasted pig."

It was fair to say that Margery and Cinders had never really got on. Margery thought little girls should be prim and proper and enjoy lady-like, polite activities like brushing their hair, sitting quietly, and possibly taking a short nap in the afternoon. Cinders was neither prim nor proper. Cinders liked to play outside and get her clothes dirty, and she never, ever brushed her hair properly. That said, Margery was prepared to overlook what a terrible disappointment her stepdaughter had been when the prince chose her to be his bride. At the time, she couldn't for the life of her fathom why he had picked that little ruffian to be a princess, but now it all made sense. She was definitely a witch and had put him under some sort of spell.

"Oh, Prince Joderick!" Margery sat up and nodded at Elly to grab the plate of cookies from the table. "Where are my manners? This must have been so hard for you. Would you like a snack? Perhaps something to drink?"

"I wouldn't mind a glass of water, if that's all right." The prince nodded, his stomach rumbling.

Margery gave Aggy a pinch and the girl ran off to the kitchen. "And to think you were going to marry that little witch," she said, patting the couch beside her. With the greatest of reluctance, Joderick sat down. He couldn't quite put his finger on it, but there was something off about this woman. *No wonder Cinders didn't like her*, he thought to himself.

"You must be heartbroken," Margery said sympathetically.

"Something like that," he agreed. "I'm more worried about Cinders than anything. I don't really know what's going on, but I don't believe she's a witch, no matter what my father says."

"Cinders couldn't possibly be a witch," her dad repeated, staring into space. Joderick thought he looked awfully pale.

"Now here's the thing," Margery said as the prince took a glass of water from Aggy and a cookie from Elly. "You say Cinders has been exiled?"

"That's right."

"And you say she rode off into the Dark Forest?"

"She did."

Joderick took a big bite of the cookie. Ew. Raisins. He was an excellent baker and this was definitely not an excellent cookie.

"But what's to stop her from coming back here?" Margery asked, suddenly looking very frightened. She grabbed both of her daughters by the collars of their pink, frilly dresses and held them so tight that Aggy's eyes began to bulge out of their sockets. "What if she returns to the cottage to cast spells on my beautiful daughters?"

Beautiful is pushing it a bit, Joderick thought, eyeing the two girls with their perfectly curled hair and high, high heels. Mostly, they just looked uncomfortable.

"I think we should come back to the palace with you," Margery said. "It's the only way to keep my daughters safe."

"We're going to live at the palace?" Elly gasped with bright, excited eyes.

"Only until we're certain that Cinders is never, ever, *ever* coming back," her mother replied, completely ignoring her grief-stricken husband.

"I'm sure Prince Joderick will keep us safe," Aggy said, gazing at the prince with big eyes. "He's so strong and brave."

Said prince gulped hard and took a big sip of water.

"That sounds lovely," he said, "but I'm not sure there's room."

"There's plenty of room—it's a palace," Margery replied dismissively. "Elly, Aggy, go and pack a bag. We must leave tonight. Before that witch comes back home."

"Cinders couldn't possibly be a witch," repeated her husband in rather a weak voice. "She's the double of her mother, and her mother was no witch, believe me. Quite the opposite, in fact. I must go and find Cinders."

Joderick turned his attention to the older man, kneeling down beside his chair. "Excuse me for saying so, sir, but I'm not sure it's a terribly good idea for you to go off into the Dark Forest. It's awfully dangerous."

"There's a very good chance she's already been eaten," added Margery. "The prince is right. You must come to the palace with us where you'll be safe."

"Absolutely not," Cinders's father said, using all his strength to stand upright. "I will not leave my little girl alone in that forest. If it's the last thing I do, I'll find her and bring her home safely. Then we'll explain everything to the king."

Margery lifted an eyebrow. "Explain what exactly?" she asked.

"It's my own fault," Cinders's father whispered to Joderick. "I never should have kept it a secret."

Joderick looked at the frail man. He seemed to have aged fifty years since the first time they'd met—there was no way he could ride off into the Dark Forest.

"I think we should all go back to the palace," Joderick suggested.

Margery, Elly, and Aggy cheered.

"And then I will go into the Dark Forest to find Cinders," he added bravely. "I'm the prince. I'll be safer."

Margery, Elly, and Aggy gasped.

"Are you . . . sure?" said Cinders's father.

"Yes," said Joderick.

"Very well. I would like to go myself, but . . . my strength is not what it was. You will make a great king one day," said Cinders's dad.

"Not if he gets eaten by a munklepoop, he won't," Margery pointed out.

Joderick took another bite of his hard, dry cookie. *If a munklepoop comes after me, I can just throw this at its head and knock it out cold*, he thought. But he didn't repeat this out loud—he'd been raised to be polite, even when people didn't deserve it.

"We'll find Cinders," he said to her father. "I promise."

Chapter Four

THE NEXT MORNING, CINDERS woke up to sunlight streaming in through the window, the sound of Sparks snoring gently beside her, and three not-at-all-happy-looking bears standing in the doorway of the bedroom.

"Who's been sleeping in my bed?" the largest bear roared.

"Not this again," said a medium-sized bear, who was wearing a very fetching floral sundress. "You can see very well who's been

sleeping in your bed. It's a human boy. He's still there."

"Good golly gosh!" Cinders cried, suddenly wide awake. "We're so sorry. We were riding through the woods, and it was late and—"

But the largest bear didn't want to hear it. He tore the duvet from Hansel's bed with a huge paw. "This is my house, this is my bed, and I shall EAT YOU UP!"

"Five more minutes, Cinders," Hansel muttered, rolling over and planting his face in the pillow.

"No, I think it's time to get up now," she said as she grabbed his hat from the bedside table.

"I cannot believe this is happening again," the mommy bear muttered. "Didn't I tell you to check the lock before we left? Do I have to do everything around here?"

"I did check the lock," the other bear said, planting his hands on his hips indignantly. "They clearly broke in."

The littlest bear, who was still just a baby, ambled over to his bed, where Sparks was hiding under the covers, and began to give the dog a good, firm pat. A little bit too firm for Sparks's liking.

"Um . . . excuse me." Cinders held up her hand to politely get the bears' attention. "Not to cause an argument, but the door was definitely unlocked."

"I knew it," sighed the mommy bear. "Look, Frank, just admit you didn't lock the door."

"Karen, do not look at me like that. I

definitely did," the larger bear argued, even though he didn't sound as if he was quite so sure. "Whatever—they still need to learn a lesson so I'm STILL GOING TO EAT THEM!"

"Daddy, no!" The baby bear grabbed hold of Sparks and squeezed him tight against his chest. "Please don't eat the doggy."

Sparks let out a strangled woof in support of the baby bear's request.

"Please don't eat us," Cinders said. "We're good people . . . Well,

I'm good, and Hansel is all right most of the time, and—"

"I'm going to interrupt you there, young lady," the mommy bear said, wagging a finger at Cinders. "This is not a hotel. What kind of person lets themselves into someone else's home in the middle of the night and sleeps in their bed?"

"And eats their porridge and breaks their chairs?" added the daddy bear.

"Um. We didn't eat any porridge," Cinders replied, a little puzzled.

"I did use quite a lot of toilet paper, but I definitely didn't break any chairs," Hansel said.

The mommy bear shook her head. She was clearly very annoyed. "My sister told me not to build a holiday home in the Dark Forest, but I wouldn't listen, would I? *It'll be peaceful*,

I said. *No one bothering you*, I said. But here you are, full of excuses, just as bad as that Goldilocks. I know she said she only came in to charge her phone, but she certainly found time to do a lot of damage. And who paid for the new chair? Muggins here, that's who."

"I think there's a very easy way to teach everyone a lesson here," the daddy bear said. "I'm going to EAT THEM!"

The mommy bear rubbed her temples and closed her eyes. "That's your answer to everything, isn't it, Frank? The gardener charges you too much for mowing the lawn—eat him. The dry cleaner shrinks your favorite trousers—eat him. If you had your way, you'd have eaten everyone in the kingdom by now."

"Maybe we should leave," Cinders suggested.

"No one is going anywhere until I've had my breakfast!" The daddy bear roared so loud that Hansel's hat flew right off his head.

"Cinders, do something!" Hansel squealed as the daddy bear came closer.

"I wish I knew how to make everyone happy!" she yelled at the top of her voice.

And, with that, Cinders's fingers began to tingle and the golden sparks started shooting out of her hands. And then she began to feel funny all over, as if the sparks were coming from every part of her. The mommy bear and the daddy bear took a step back, but Hansel looked on with wide eyes. This was a lot more dramatic than what had happened in the forest the night before! Cinders looked as though

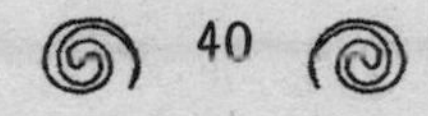

she was made entirely of fireworks.

When the magic finished, Cinders shook herself and blinked at the bears. They were staring at her in disbelief. She knew she'd done something impressive if she had stunned talking bears into silence.

The baby bear let go of Sparks and ran over to his parents, hiding behind his mom's leg.

"I say," Sparks said, sniffing hungrily. "Can anyone else smell sausages?"

Chapter Five

"CINDERS, I THINK YOUR magic is getting stronger. This has to be your most successful wish yet," declared Sparks as the three bears and the three friends sat down at the kitchen table, ready to tuck into the enormous feast that had magically appeared when Cinders made her wish.

It turned out that the one thing that made the daddy bear happy was a great big cooked breakfast, and the one thing that made the mommy bear happy was three freshly made beds and a new lock on the front door, and the one thing that made the baby bear happy was a tiny red puppy that Cinders noticed looked an awful lot like Sparks.

His first wish had been for a new phone, but that had only led to a very long conversation with his mom about how much screen time he was allowed, and so they had decided on a dog instead, and Cinders had made the wish again.

Of course the thing that made Cinders, Hansel, and Sparks happy was not being eaten by the daddy bear, and so it seemed that she really had done a splendid job.

The table was overflowing with food: sausages, bacon, eggs, beans, toast, fruit, yogurt, croissants and cakes and muffins, and other goodies. Even after everyone had eaten their fill, there was still more food left over than Cinders had ever seen in her whole life.

"You must take some with you," said the mommy bear, all smiles now that she'd eaten. "I'll pack you a lunch."

"And, of course, you're very welcome to stay, if you'd like," the daddy bear said as he licked his paws clean. "Perhaps not in our beds, but we've got a very nice sofa bed in the living room."

"That's very kind of you," Cinders said,

holding her hand out in front of Hansel's face before he could accept the invitation, "but we really must be getting on. My fairy godmother told me the journey to Fairyland might be tricky, and we really should set off as early as we can."

"She wasn't wrong about that," the daddy bear said. "This forest is perfect if you're a great big grizzly bear looking for a quiet weekend away, but it's not the kind of place you want to hang about in if you're a delicious-looking little girl."

Cinders gulped.

"Ignore Frank," said Mommy Bear. "He's always going on about eating people, but he can't even stomach sushi, let alone uncooked humans. The quickest way to get to Fairyland is to ride due north from the cottage until you reach the Alabaster Tower. That's the halfway point between the kingdom and Fairyland."

"But, whatever you do, do not go into the Alabaster Tower," warned Daddy Bear.

"Why's that?" asked Sparks, casually snaffling another sausage from the table.

"No one who goes in has ever come back out again," Mommy Bear replied. "In fact, I can't remember the last time anyone went off as far as the tower and returned home."

Cinders looked down at her no-longer-sparkly fingers. It didn't matter. She'd always known the quest would be dangerous, and it wasn't as though she could go home anyway. The king would lock her up in the dungeons for the rest of her life.

"We'll be okay," she said, trying to convince everyone at the table, including herself. "And we really ought to be setting off before it gets any later. Thank you so much for having us. Come on, Hansel. Ready, Sparks?"

"I've been thinking," said Hansel as he followed her out into the garden. "What if your fairy godmother isn't telling you the truth?"

Cinders gave him a stern look. "Brian wouldn't lie," she replied, grinning at Mouse as he trotted around in happy circles, crumbs of cheese sticking to his horse-mouse whiskers. "She's my fairy godmother."

"But what if she isn't," Hansel said as Sparks came bounding down the path, carrying a knapsack absolutely bursting with food, waving goodbye to the three bears. "What if the king is right and the fairies are evil and she's trying to trick you for some reason?"

"Hansel," Cinders said very slowly. "Fairies aren't evil just because the king says they are. After all, my mom was a fairy and she was good."

Hansel scratched his head before pulling his hat down over his ears. He'd been brought up to believe all magic was bad, but here was wish-granting Cinders and her talking dog, and they were his friends. Maybe she was right.

"If you don't want to come to Fairyland, Sparks and Mouse and I will go on without you," Cinders said, tossing her messy hair over her shoulder. What she wouldn't have given for a scrunchie. "You can find your way back home on your own."

Hmm. Hansel really didn't want to trek back through the Dark Forest alone, and he definitely didn't want to go home and explain to his mom why he'd been pinching gingerbread tiles off the neighbor's roof again. But he also didn't want to get lost in the forest. Ooh, gingerbread! Now there was an idea . . .

"What if we left a trail of breadcrumbs behind us?" Hansel suggested.

Cinders crossed her arms and looked at Hansel like he was mad. "Breadcrumbs?"

"Yes," he replied, grabbing one of the slightly stale gingerbread tiles from his bag. "To mark the trail. In case we need to . . . turn around."

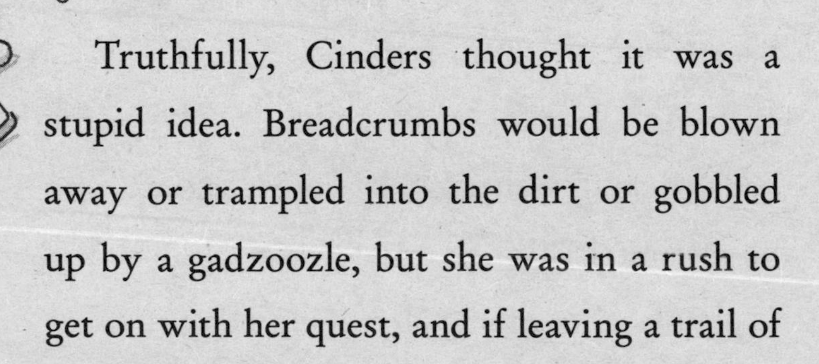

Truthfully, Cinders thought it was a stupid idea. Breadcrumbs would be blown away or trampled into the dirt or gobbled up by a gadzoozle, but she was in a rush to get on with her quest, and if leaving a trail of breadcrumbs made Hansel happy, then that's what they would do.

"Breadcrumbs it is," she said with a huff, clambering onto Mouse's back. "Now let's get going."

"You'll see," Hansel whispered to Sparks. "Just wait until we need to find our way back here and have to follow my trail. Then she'll eat her words."

Sparks smiled and bounded on ahead as Hansel climbed up behind Cinders. He was pretty sure the birds in the forest would be eating the breadcrumbs before Cinders ate her words, but he didn't say anything. Why ruin Hansel's good mood?

Chapter Six

EVEN THOUGH HIS ENTIRE world had been turned upside down since the ball, there was one thing Prince Joderick knew for certain. He should never have brought Cinders's stepmother and her stepsisters to the palace. Ever since they'd arrived, they had not left him alone. Margery insisted they all ride together in their coach to "let the poor prince rest" and, once they arrived, she convinced the king to allow her daughters to sit on either side of the prince at dinner "for protection." He couldn't even sneak off to the bathroom without one of them waiting for him when he came out. He didn't know how Cinders had survived living with them for so long. If he had to stay under the same roof as them for another second, he had a feeling he might start shooting sparks out of his fingertips as well.

"Oh, there you are!"

Cripes, they'd found him again!

"Um . . . good morning, um . . . Which one are you again?" Joderick asked, flattening himself against the stone wall of the hallway.

"Oh, you are funny." The girl laughed as she twirled her hair around her finger. "I'm Agnes. My sister, Elly, has dull, dishwater-brown hair. Mine is a more glossy, chocolatey mahogany color."

The palace had, at last count, 347 rooms and it still was not big enough for Joderick and the sisters.

"Right, noted," he replied with a tight smile. "Bathroom's all yours."

"I was actually looking for you," Agnes said, looking down at her toes. "I thought perhaps you might like to accompany me on a walk around the gardens."

Joderick could not think of anything he would like less.

"That sounds like a real treat," he said, "but unfortunately I've got some things to attend to."

"Oh?" Agnes looked curious. "What kind of things?"

"Very boring prince things," he replied. "That I have to do alone."

"Wow!" Agnes looked impressed. That or she had a bad tummy ache, he couldn't be sure. "Shall I wait for you and we can go for a walk later?"

"No!" shouted Joderick before recovering his princely manners. "I mean, it might take me a while, and I wouldn't want to keep you waiting. Why don't you go for a walk with your mother? Or your sister? Or, better yet, both of them? A very, very long walk."

"Joderick, you're so funny," she tittered, covering her mouth with her hand even though he hadn't made a joke at all. "Perhaps I'll go and see what the queen is doing. Last night she told me she'd always wanted a daughter like me."

Agnes gave him a wink and swept away down the hallway.

"Cripes almighty," he muttered, pulling at his collar. It felt very tight all of a sudden. When he was sure she was gone, Joderick opened the door to his father's private chambers and let himself in.

Even though he had lived in the palace all his life, the prince had never, ever been inside the king's private chambers on his own. But this was an emergency—he had to help Cinders and her father. No matter what he had heard about fairies and witches, he simply couldn't believe his new friend was up to no good. How could someone so kind and funny and brave and clever be bad? Whatever the case, he had promised her father he would go into the Dark Forest and bring her back, and Joderick believed that promises were made to be kept.

But how to find Cinders when she was already far ahead of him in the Dark Forest? Thankfully, Jodders had a plan. When he was very little, his father had taken him into his chambers and shown him a map of what lay beyond the boundaries of the kingdom, but he hadn't seen it in more than ten years.

"Now, if I was a map to Fairyland," Joderick muttered to himself, looking around the forbidden room, "where would I be?"

The king's private chambers were very, very fancy. It wasn't necessarily how Joderick would have decorated, but he had to admit that it was very imposing and impressive in a kingly sort of way. Lots of red velvet drapes covered

the windows, and there was huge wooden furniture that didn't look comfortable at all. As well as an awful lot of animal heads. Joderick preferred his animals running around outside rather than stuffed and mounted on a wall.

He hated attending meetings with his parents in this room and much preferred the hustle and bustle of the kitchens, all steamy and shouty, with Chef singing and Cook swearing and tray upon tray of sweet treats just waiting to be tasted.

When he was king, he would hold all his meetings with his advisers around the big kitchen table at six a.m., just when the bread came out of the oven. That was when the kitchen smelled the absolute best.

In one corner of the room, he spotted the chest where his father kept all the maps of the kingdom, but Joderick knew the map he wanted wasn't in there. He'd been through that chest a million times, planning adventurous rides that would take him all over the land, even though he hardly ever left the palace grounds and never ever on his own. He was quite sure that the chest wasn't where his father would hide anything especially secret.

Perhaps it's underneath something, he pondered, thinking back to the first time he'd met Cinders. They had both been hiding underneath a table at the palace ball. Underneath was a brilliant place to hide something if you didn't want anyone to find it.

First he looked beneath his father's chair, but there wasn't anything there. Then he looked under the table where all the king's advisers sat when they were advising him. Nothing. All that left was his father's desk.

Hmm. "No drawers, no slots, no holes, no nothing," Joderick muttered as he crawled under the massive piece of furniture on his hands and knees and inspected the bottom.

The desk was so big, his father almost disappeared when he sat behind it. The king had once told him his grandfather's grandfather had had it built especially for him. Joderick had to assume his great-grandfather's grandfather had been a good deal taller than his father.

Flat on his back, Joderick blew the hair out of his face and stared up at the underside of the desk. Then he saw it. The tiniest, tiniest hint of a crack in one of the huge legs. Three of the desk's legs were smooth, shiny, and solid. Whole tree trunks, his father had told him, chopped down in the Dark Forest and polished until they shone like onyx. But one of the legs, the back left leg to be precise, had a line running all the way down from top to bottom. Joderick ran his thumb along it, just to make sure he wasn't seeing things. But, sure enough, the crack was there. And, when he gave the leg a knock, it sounded hollow.

Glancing at the door to make sure he was still alone, he gave the leg another good, hard knock, and as if by magic (only not, because—as we all know—his father didn't agree with magic) a secret compartment sprang open. Reaching inside, Joderick felt something soft and something crisp—parchment! And . . . something wrapped in silk?

It had to be the map,
it just had to be!

Chapter Seven

WHEN THE THREE BEARS told Cinders to head due north from their cottage, she'd assumed that meant the Alabaster Tower must be quite close by, but, after several hours of riding, they still hadn't seen anything other than tree after tree after tree after tree.

"I don't want to make myself unpopular," Sparks said, raising one red, bushy eyebrow, "but we seem to have been riding for an awfully long time and I don't think we're getting any closer to Fairyland."

"We definitely are," Cinders replied. "We're riding due north, the breadcrumb trail is behind us, and any second now we're going to see the Alabaster Tower. Then we'll be halfway!"

"I wonder what the three bears are doing," Hansel said, peeking up into the trees above. They hadn't seen the sun in ages. "What do you think they're having for their tea? Do you think they made any extra?"

"Why don't I try another wish?" Cinders suggested. "Just to hurry things along."

They were definitely on the right track, she could feel it, but maybe a little magical confirmation would set their minds at ease.

She pulled Mouse's reins gently and hopped

down to the ground. *The Dark Forest really is very dark*, she thought to herself. *Whoever had named it would not win any prizes for originality.*

“Okay, here goes . . .” She closed her eyes and wiggled her fingers to warm them up. “I wish someone would show us the way to the Alabaster Tower.”

Very, very slowly, her fingers began to tingle. Cinders watched as her nails turned very slightly silver. And then everything stopped.

“Well, that was disappointing,” Sparks said.

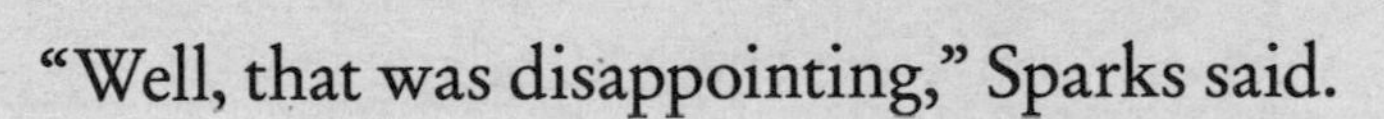

“I don’t know what’s wrong,” Cinders said, concentrating as hard as she could. “It was a clear wish, wasn't it? And I've eaten so much cake!"

"More than anyone else, actually," her doggy pal pointed out.

"Cake makes my magic stronger," Cinders reminded him. "I have to eat it."

"I wish I was magic," Hansel said with a moan, sliding down from Mouse's back and stretching his arms above his head. "I flippin' love cake."

"Let me try again," said Cinders, shaking herself. "I wish someone would show us the way to the Alabaster Tower."

She closed her eyes and waited. And waited. And waited. But nothing happened.

"Er . . . Cinders?" Sparks muttered.

"Sparks, be quiet—I'm trying to concentrate," she said, squeezing her eyes shut even tighter.

"I realize that, but I think we need to be moving on . . ."

"I know I can do it if I focus," Cinders whispered, more to herself than anyone else.

Focusing had never been a particular skill of hers. Climbing trees? Sure. Swimming in the river? She was an ace. But concentrating on one thing at a time? Not Cinders's speciality.

"I do appreciate that," woofed her friend, "but it's definitely time for us to get going!"

"Sparks!" Cinders grumbled crossly. "Will you just give me a minute?"

"Cinders!" Hansel bellowed at the top of his voice. "There's a munklepoop behind you!"

Opening her eyes, Cinders turned to come face-to-face with something she had never seen before and hoped never to see again. It was very, very, very big, almost as tall as the trees, and shaped somewhat like a foot, only it was covered in matted bright-blue fur and had blazing yellow eyes and—oh, yes! There were the claws! Why did it have to have claws? It already had very long, very pointy teeth—the claws were almost a little too much. It was the scariest thing Cinders had ever laid eyes on, and that included her stepmother before she'd had her first cup of tea in the morning.

"I always wondered what a munklepoop would look like up close," Sparks whispered, all four legs shaking as the munklepoop began to creep closer, claws scraping along the forest

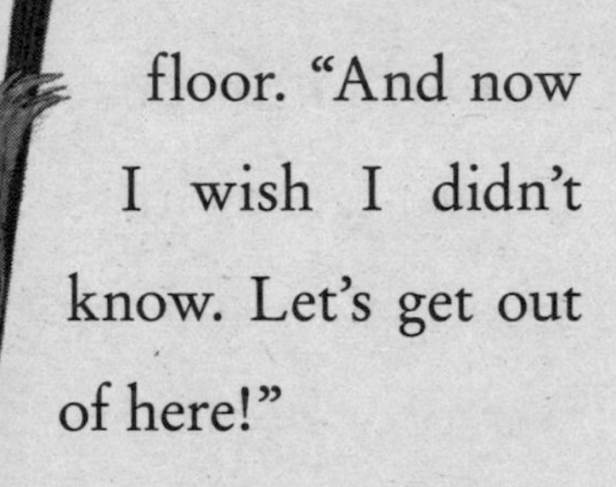

floor. "And now I wish I didn't know. Let's get out of here!"

As quick as a flash, Cinders grabbed Sparks under one arm and leaped up onto Mouse's back. "Everyone on!" she yelled, taking Hansel's hand and hauling him up behind her. "Is he following us?" she asked, cracking the reins.

"GRRRARGGH!" growled the munkle-poop as it leaped high off the ground and landed so close that Sparks could smell its breath. It most certainly hadn't brushed its teeth that morning.

"I'll take that as a yes," Cinders said with a grimace as Mouse set off at lightning speed, the munklepoop roaring as it chased after them.

Chapter Eight

JODERICK PEERED INTO THE hole in the desk leg. He could see several objects hidden in there. Precious objects, obviously, otherwise why bother hiding them?

He pulled out the soft silky thing first, a carefully wrapped package tied up in a square of pale gray silk. Inside the parcel was a letter and a small painting of a woman wearing a crown. They both felt very old, as though

they might turn into dust if he wasn't careful. The parchment had already turned yellow and curled up at the edges, and it was written in a language Joderick didn't recognize. But the woman in the painting looked awfully familiar.

She looked just like Cinders.

She had the same green eyes, the same light hair, the same happy smile. If Cinders ever thought to brush her hair, it could have been her double.

Joderick carefully folded the painting back in the silk square and placed it in his pocket before reaching back into the secret compartment. He didn't know who this woman was, but he was certainly going to find out. The next thing he found was much bigger and seemed to be stuck. He tugged, as carefully as he could, determined to get the parchment out into the light so he could take a look at it.

"It's got to be the map," he muttered, reaching even deeper into the desk leg until he was in all the way up to his elbow.

Just as he was about to pull his arm out and try again, Joderick heard a loud creak.

Someone was outside the door! There was only one thing to do. He gave the parchment a big, strong tug.

R-R-I-I-I-I-I-I-I-I-I-I-P-P-P-P-P-P!

Joderick fell backward, a huge piece of dusty paper in his hands. It was the map! There was the palace, the Dark Forest, and the mountains beyond, just as he remembered from when he was little.

Whoever was outside the door was chatting very loudly. Dillydallying was one of his father's very favorite pastimes, but Joderick knew he might not have very long and the map was very large. He folded it this way and that, but he couldn't fit it in his pocket.

"When I'm king, all maps will be pocket-sized," he muttered as the handle of the door slowly turned. Quickly, Joderick rolled up the map and shoved it in the only place he could think of. His pants.

Sprinting out of the room, he flew right past the king and a whole host of advisers.

"Joderick Jorenson Picklebottom! What were you doing in my private chambers?" the king cried as his son raced away.

"Um . . . I thought I heard someone inside," he panted, thinking quickly. "I wanted to make sure it wasn't another witch. But it's all right—there's no one in there."

"Ah, truly Prince Joderick is a fine, brave boy," said one

of the advisers, stroking his long gray beard as Jodders disappeared from view.

"He'll make a great king one day," agreed another, nodding sagely.

"Does he usually carry things around in his royal britches?" asked a third.

But Joderick wasn't listening. He was already racing down the stairs to the stables.

Chapter Nine

"I THINK THE MUNKLEPOOP IS hungry!" Sparks said, peeking out from under one paw as the monster chased them through the trees, tearing them up by the roots as it pounded ever closer. "And I do not want to be on the menu."

"Sparks, give me all your sausages!" yelled Hansel as the big, furry beast bounded after them. For something so very large, it was very, very, very fast.

“Not the time for a snack, Hansel!” the dog woofed back.

“Not for me!” he shouted. “Hand over that knapsack!”

With the utmost reluctance, Sparks passed Hansel his bag, nudging him toward the half dozen sausages Sparks had hidden at the bottom.

“I hope you know what you’re doing!” Cinders cried as she squeezed Mouse with her knees, his hooves thundering along the floor of the forest. Branches and leaves flashed by her face as they galloped on, with no idea where they were heading.

“Here you go, Munkles! Eat your fill!” Hansel shouted, hurling the sausages at the slavering creature as hard as he could.

The munklepoop ignored the first sausage,

his bright-blue fur almost a blur as he ran faster and faster and faster. But Hansel's second pork missile hit the monster right between the eyes and he skidded to a halt. He sniffed the sausage for a moment before lapping it up with his spiky purple tongue.

"It's working!" Hansel said with a whoop. "He's eating the sausage!"

Without a second's hesitation, Hansel launched the rest of the sausages in the munkle-poop's general direction until he was all out of sausages and the big blue ball of terror had enough snacks to keep him distracted while the friends made their escape.

"Hansel, you totally saved the day," Cinders gasped as Mouse dashed on through the forest.

"Yes, but at what cost?" Sparks said with a sniff. All those sausages—gone forever.

"No need to sound so surprised, Cinders," Hansel said, his chest puffed out with pride, his stomach full of butterflies, and just a little bit out of breath. "Can we slow down now? I don't think he's coming after us. And my stomach feels a bit weird."

"Okay," Cinders replied, pulling Mouse's

reins in just a tad. She didn't want to be eaten by a munklepoop, but she also didn't want Hansel to puke on her either. "I still can't figure out why my wish didn't work. Anyone got any ideas?"

"Nope, but would you look at that?" Hansel tapped her on the shoulder and pointed through the trees to a building dead ahead. "What do you reckon it is?"

"Um . . . let me see," Cinders replied, a smile spreading slowly across her face. "It's a tall, bright-white structure. Do you think it could be the Alabaster Tower?"

Hmm. Maybe her magic hadn't completely deserted her. After all, she had asked some-one to show her how to get to the tower and, in a funny sort of way, that was what the munklepoop had done.

"Perhaps next time you could specify exactly who you'd like to give us directions," Sparks said, eyeing the sparkling tower in the distance. "Because I'd rather not take travel advice from a munklepoop again."

"Fair enough," Cinders said, giving him a happy scratch behind the ear. "Can you believe we're halfway to Fairyland?"

"No," he said with a sigh, "but I can believe we're completely out of sausages."

Cinders grinned and rode on with the Alabaster Tower in her sights, another step closer to finding the answers to her questions.

Chapter Ten

THE SUN WAS BEGINNING to droop in the afternoon sky when Joderick found himself in the Dark Forest. After nabbing the map, he'd had to hide behind a suit of armor for a whole thirty minutes while Elly and Aggy called his name.

"Those girls are like a cold draft," he muttered to his horse, Muffin. "They get everywhere."

The horse neighed in seeming agreement,

but one thing she didn't agree with was the idea of riding off into the Dark Forest. What was Prince Joderick thinking? Did he really expect her to leave the royal stables, with the best hay and the nicest apples, to gallop off into this nightmare? She might not have been a magic horse like Mouse, but she wasn't stupid.

She stepped backward, uneasy, as Joderick tried to encourage her on.

"I know this isn't the sort of thing we usually do," he said, "but we've got to help Cinders."

Muffin snorted. Did they really?

A rustling in the trees made them both start and, for just a moment, Joderick wasn't quite sure why he was doing this. He didn't like girls all that much, and he'd only met Cinders a few days ago! Now here he was, running off into the Dark Forest, the one place he'd been forbidden to enter by his father. It seemed like a very un-Joderick-like thing to do. He'd much rather be baking a cake in the kitchens or taking Muffin for a lovely ride through town to visit some friends. But he had a funny feeling inside that something was wrong and that Cinders needed his help.

His father had been acting very strangely, even for him. (He was always a little odd.) The secret compartment, the map, the letter, the painting, exiling Cinders before anyone bothered to ask what was going on? All weird. Joderick had been so sure fairies and magic were bad, but meeting Cinders had changed all that, and he knew in his heart that if he was in trouble she would try to help him.

"What kind of prince would I be if I didn't try to save her?" Joderick asked Muffin. "Not a very good one, that's for sure."

Muffin gave another snort. Being honorable and brave was all well and good, but what if she missed her dinner?

"We can do this, Muffin," he said, shaking her reins and taking a deep breath. "All the princes in my books go on grand adventures. And this will be quite the adventure."

With a whinny and a neigh, Muffin finally gave in. If Prince Joderick wanted to ride into the Dark Forest right before teatime, then she would ride into the Dark Forest and teatime would have to wait. But she did rather hope they'd be back before supper.

Chapter Eleven

DEEPER IN THE DARK Forest, Cinders was starting to get a little frustrated. It felt as though they'd been riding toward the Alabaster Tower for hours, but they never seemed to get any closer!

"Are you absolutely certain we aren't riding around in circles?" Sparks asked as kindly as he could. Which wasn't that kindly because he was still quite sore about Hansel throwing all his sausages at the munklepoop.

"We can't be," Hansel replied. "We'd have seen my breadcrumb trail by now."

"Unless something is eating the breadcrumbs," Sparks muttered, his tummy grumbling rather loudly.

"Would you like a bite of my brownie?" Cinders said, hoping he wouldn't really want it, seeing as it was her last one.

Sparks shook his head and she sighed with relief before taking a great big bite.

"It is weird," she said through a chocolatey mouthful. "We've been riding for ages, but the tower looks farther away than ever. I wish I knew what was going on."

"Cinders!" Hansel yelped, searching all around

for munklepoops as his friend's fingers began to tingle and glow. "How many times do we have to remind you to be careful what you wish for?"

"Don't panic," Cinders said, bringing Mouse to a standstill as sparks shot out of her fingers. No trouble with her magic this time. "It's not munklepoops. Look!"

Down on the ground, right in front of them, a little pink puffball with big eyes, a smiley face, short arms, and little legs appeared out of nowhere. It came up no higher than Cinders's

knee and right away she noticed, in its arms, a huge pile of gingerbread crumbs.

"Oi!" Cinders shouted, hopping down from her horse. "What are you doing with those?"

The fluffy pink creature paused for a second, staring open-mouthed at the girl as she marched over.

"What's wrong?" Cinders asked. "Can't you hear me?"

"I can hear you all right," the thing squeaked. "But a better question would be, can you see me?"

"I most certainly can," she replied.

"Crumbs!" the creature whispered, dropping its precious load of gingerbread in surprise.

"Exactly," Cinders agreed. "Now, do you want to tell me what's going on here?"

Chapter Twelve

"**WE'RE NOT GOING TO** hurt you," Cinders said as she sat down next to the little creature. It was trembling, its pale-pink fur puffed out on end. "I'm Cinders, and these are my friends—Hansel, Sparks, and Mouse."

"Mouse?"

"He's a horse," she answered. "It's a long story."

"He was a mouse and then Cinders wished he was a horse and then he never turned back

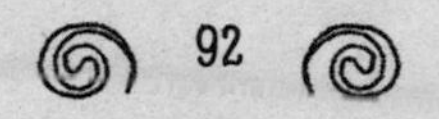

properly," Hansel called.

"Not that long a story then," the pink puffball said.

"I suppose not," Cinders said with a shrug. "So what's your name?" She smiled at the furry little thing as it gave her a suspicious look. *It really was very cute,* she thought to herself. Definitely superior to munklepoops and grumpy bears as far as creatures of the Dark Forest went.

"My name is Bloop," it said eventually. "Pleased to meet you."

"Pleased to meet you too," said Cinders. She held out her hand to shake, but Bloop took a step backward and stared at her as though she was weird. *Not a handshaker*, she noted. That was fine. "And not to be rude," she added, "but what exactly are you?"

"Me?" Bloop replied, eyes wide with astonishment. "I'm a blobble, of course. Isn't it obvious?"

"Not really," said Cinders. "Sorry."

"I don't think I've ever even heard of a blobble before," said Sparks.

"I suppose that makes sense." Bloop gave a wise nod. "We're usually invisible to everyone but our owners."

"But . . . we don't own you," said Cinders.

"I know," said Bloop. "It's all a bit strange."

"And what are you doing here?" Cinders asked, wondering if it would be all right for her to give Bloop a stroke. She'd never seen such soft fur, but she knew you weren't supposed to touch people, or blobbles, without asking permission first, and they *had* only just met.

"I belong to the royal family of, um . . . well, a place," Bloop said, casting his eyes left and right shiftily, "and my job is to protect the, er, place . . . from intruders. Which unfortunately includes you."

"Well, I never," Sparks huffed, far less interested in stroking the little pink ball of fluff, but strongly considering giving it an investigatory sniff. "Intruders? How rude!"

"We're not intruders," Cinders insisted. "We're questers. We're on a quest to find Fairyland, and we're looking for the Alabaster Tower. Can you help us, Bloop?"

At that, Bloop's eyes grew very, very wide. "I'm afraid I can't tell you anything unless you know the secret password. Very sorry—you seem perfectly nice—but rules is rules," he said, collecting his spilled breadcrumbs as quickly as he could. "Nice to meet you all. A horse that used to be a mouse, eh? What will they think of next?"

"Wait!" Cinders cried. "Please don't leave!"

But it was too late. As quickly as he had appeared, Bloop the blobble vanished, leaving the four of them all alone in the woods.

“Oh, flipping fiddlesticks!” Cinders sobbed, a big fat tear falling down her cheek.

“Now, now,” Sparks chided. “No need for that sort of language.”

“No need?” she replied, spinning around in the dirt with tears running down her face. “No need? Sparks, there’s every need! We’re tired, we’re hungry, we almost got eaten by a miffed bear and a munklepoop, and now some flipping pink puffball has nicked our bread-crumbs so we have no idea where we’re going or how to get home. I’m starting to think this whole thing was a terrible idea. We should have stayed in the palace and let the king lock me up in the dungeons for all the use I’ve been. Some quester I’ve turned out to be.”

“That’s it, young lady!” Sparks barked, his fur positively bristling.

Cinders blinked at her lifelong puppy pal. Was he shouting at her? When she was sad?

"I'm not having this!" Sparks went on. He was definitely shouting. "We've no time for you to sit around feeling sorry for yourself. It's been a big week, I'll grant you. You've found out you're half fairy and have magical powers, you've met the prince, moved to the palace, been exiled by King Pickle-bottom, rescued Hansel, avoided being eaten by assorted animals, and now you've met your first blobble."

"It's pretty incredible when you think about it," Hansel mumbled to Mouse, who squeaked in agreement.

"What of it?" Cinders sniffed. She still felt like a failure.

"You want to give up because a pile of breadcrumbs has disappeared?" Sparks barked. "I've known you since you were born and I am not standing for this nonsense. It's time to pull up your socks and find another way to Fairyland. I will not let you give up, Cinderella!"

Cinders gave a big gulp. People only used her full name when she really was in trouble.

Before anyone could say anything else, Bloop the blobble reappeared with a pop and a flash, plopping to the ground between the girl and her dog.

"Giddy gadkins," he said, looking at them with great curiosity. "Did one of you just use the secret password?"

"I don't think so," Cinders said, wiping away her tears with the back of her hand. "We don't know what it is, remember?"

"That's funny. I was sure I heard someone say Cinderella." He clapped his hand over his mouth quickly. "Not that Cinderella means anything, obviously."

"No, we did say that," Cinders said, frowning. "Sparks said it. Cinderella is my full name."

"That is very odd," Bloop said, scratching his head. "Because Cinderella is the secret password to the Alabaster Tower, as decreed by the royal family of Fairyland. Since you know it, I can take you to the tower right now, if you'd like?"

“Good golly gosh,” whispered Cinders. “What do you think that means?”

“I really couldn’t say,” Sparks replied before giving his friend a big, loving lick on the cheek. “Shall we go and find out?”

Chapter Thirteen

BACK IN THE PALACE was another royal family, and they weren't nearly as delighted to hear the name Cinderella.

King Picklebottom was sitting on his throne with the queen at his side, awaiting an update on the missing girl. Margery, Elly, and Aggy sat silently in tall wooden chairs that had been pushed up against the walls. *Not quite thrones, but close enough for now,* Margery had thought to herself. It was only a matter of time before Joderick fell head over heels in love with one of her daughters, and then they'd all live in the palace forever, happily ever after.

Elly was about to suggest a quick afternoon game of I Spy to break the tension when the door to the throne room burst open. One of the king's absolute favorite soldiers (mostly because he always kept his armor extra shiny) entered with a very worried look on his face.

"Is she back?" cried the king, rising to his feet.

"She is not, Your Highness," said the soldier, "and I'm afraid I have some more not-altogether-brilliant news."

"If you're going to tell me that Cook is out of ice cream, you can turn right back around," the king huffed. "It's Tuesday and on Tuesday we have ice cream. Today has been bad enough already."

"In that case, I've got good news and bad news," the soldier replied.

"Good news first," King Picklebottom demanded.

"The good news is that Cook has three different kinds of ice cream," he said. "Chocolate, vanilla, and floople blossom."

"Hmm," said the king. "I like floople blossom so that *is* good news. And the bad news?"

The soldier gulped. "Prince Joderick is missing."

The queen SHRIEKED at the top of her lungs while Elly and Aggy fainted clean away.

"What do you mean he's *missing*?" bellowed the king. "He'll be hiding in the kitchens or running around the gardens or getting up to something he shouldn't as per usual."

"I'm afraid not," the soldier said, scratching his shiny silver helmet. "One of my guards spotted him entering the Dark Forest a little while ago."

"But that's preposterous!" shouted King Picklebottom. He really was a very loud man. "I saw him only this morning when he was coming out of . . ."

And that was when he remembered. Joderick had been hurrying out of his private chambers. Looking shifty. With something hidden down his britches.

"Just a mo!" The king jumped off his throne and sprinted down the corridor, throwing open the doors to his chambers before his guards could even catch up with him. Plopping down onto the floor (not an altogether easy task when wearing a full ermine-trimmed robe), he twisted open the secret compartment in the leg of his desk and reached inside. All that was left was half a sheet of parchment. His secret map to Fairyland had been ripped in two—Joderick must have torn it without realizing.

Even worse—the letter and the painting were both missing. The last thing his father ever told him was to protect the map and hide the painting. This was not good news at all.

"Oh dear," he muttered to himself. "Oh dear, oh dear indeed."

Looking up, he saw everyone from the throne room gathered around the doorway.

"You!" King Picklebottom cried, pointing at Margery. "Your daughter cast a spell on my son!"

"Stepdaughter," Margery replied, realizing she was in trouble. Without another word, she fell to her knees before the king and grabbed hold of his ankles as she wept. "I fear it is true, Your Highness. Cinders has cast a spell on us all!" she wailed, forcing out a few fake tears for good measure. "But please, you must take pity on us. We were living under her spell as well. Even our home isn't safe. The palace is the only place we can be protected from that little monster."

"Bit harsh," whispered Aggy.

"Stay out of it," Elly whispered back.

"All right, that's quite enough of that," the king said, shaking the woman off his ankles. As annoying as she was, he had a sneaking

suspicion she was cleverer than she was letting on, and the last thing he needed was her getting a look at his half map and asking questions.

No one needed to know about the letter or the painting. Ever.

"Her father must know something," he declared. "Bring him to me at once."

"My husband has been terribly ill ever since we arrived here," Margery explained,

before lowering her voice to a whisper and wiping away an invisible tear. "I believe it's another spell cast by his wicked daughter."

The king paced back and forth, trying not to panic. On the one hand, he was very happy to leave Cinders in the Dark Forest to be gobbled up by nobbledizooks, but, on the other, he very much wanted Joderick back, even if he had stolen half his map.

"Joderick would never disobey me and enter the Dark Forest unless he had been bewitched," the king decided, thinking out loud. "Therefore I reverse my decree."

"Which one?" asked his first adviser.

"The one I made yesterday," the king said.

"The one about no one wearing yellow on Fridays?" asked the second adviser.

"No!" yelled the king. "The other one!"

"The one about everyone wearing yellow on Saturdays?" asked a third.

"The one about Cinderella's exile!" the king bawled. Honestly, you just couldn't get good staff these days. "The girl is no longer exiled. She must be returned to the palace and bring Prince Joderick with her."

"But who is going to go into the Dark Forest to find her?" asked the king's favorite soldier. He tried to cross his fingers behind his back, hoping very much that it wouldn't be him, but it was almost impossible to cross your fingers while wearing a gauntlet.

The king climbed back onto his throne, his mind made up.

"There's only one person I can trust," he said with a dark look on his wrinkly face. "Get me the Huntsman."

Chapter Fourteen

HANSEL DID NOT LIKE the look of the Alabaster Tower one little bit.

It was too tall and too skinny. Imagine sweeping all the stairs that had to be inside? No, thank you. And he always ended up doing all the sweeping, no matter what. Gretel nabbed the easy jobs.

Cinders, on the other hand, was ecstatic. They were finally getting closer to Fairyland!

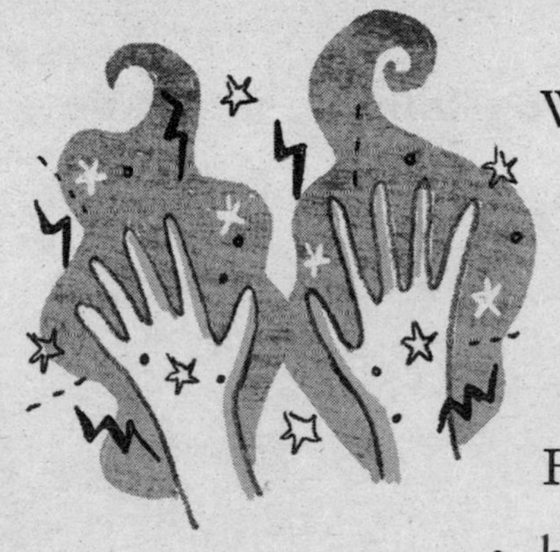

With every step they took, she felt the funny feeling in her fingers grow a little stronger. First it was a tingle, then a buzz, and eventually it felt as though she had fireworks exploding inside her hands, and she liked it very much. Brian, her fairy godmother, had said her powers would get stronger as she got closer to Fairyland, and it looked as though she'd been telling the truth.

"What do you think is inside?" Cinders asked her friends, wiggling her fingers.

“More like *who* do you think is inside,” Sparks replied, watching a spiral of white smoke drifting out of the top of the tower. “On the upside, it looks like they’ve got the kettle on.”

“I think it must be fairies,” Cinders guessed with an

extra skip in her step. "Not even my dad could build something this beautiful, and he's the best builder in the entire kingdom."

"I hope they're happy to have visitors," Hansel added gloomily. "Whoever they are."

The tall, spindly trees

of the Dark Forest began to thin out until the gang found themselves entering a clearing. In front of them was a moat and beyond the moat was the tower, glistening and glimmering in the sunlight. Cinders couldn't see a single brick or window in the entire thing. It looked as though it had been carved out of a single giant piece of crystal, with just one huge drawbridge at the front.

The only problem was the drawbridge was up and there was no one around to lower it.

"How do you reckon we get inside?" Cinders asked. "Should we swim across?"

"No way," Hansel said, peeking into the moat. "That water's got to be fifteen meters deep, and it's full of snapfizzles."

Cinders looked over his shoulder and saw he was right. Snapfizzles were the very worst kind of fish. If you didn't know better, you might think they were cute, with their big eyes and rainbow scales, but, if you got too close, they'd snap at you with their shiny teeth. Her father had told her that once a snapfizzle snaps on to you, it never, ever lets go.

"It's almost as though someone doesn't want us getting inside," Sparks noted, scratching his left ear with his hind leg. "Perhaps we ought to keep on going."

"But we have to find out which way to go next," Cinders reminded him. "The bears only told us that the Alabaster Tower was halfway. Do you want to spend another night riding around in circles?"

Mouse squeaked loudly in protest. He certainly didn't.

"If we could get over the water, I bet I

could find a way inside," Hansel said, eyeing up the tower. "If there's one thing I'm good at—"

"It's sneaking into other people's houses," Cinders finished for him.

"You say that like it's a bad thing," Hansel muttered, kicking a stone into the moat.

"If only I had wings like Brian," Cinders sighed. "Then I could fly us all over the moat."

She touched her thumb to the tips of her fingers and they crackled and fizzed. Just for a moment, she almost felt as though she didn't need wings. She almost felt as though—

"Um . . . Cinders," Sparks said, his leg freezing in mid-scratch.

"Yes?"

"Are you aware that you're floating in the air right now?"

She looked down and saw that her feet were fifteen centimeters off the grass.

"Good golly gosh!" she gasped as she fell back to earth and landed right on her behind with a bump. "Well, that was new."

Even though he didn't want to admit it, Hansel was terribly impressed. He'd always fancied flying as a magical power. He thought it might be nice to be able to zoom up into the sky and away from all your problems. Hovering fifteen centimeters off the ground wasn't going to get Cinders very far, but it was a pretty good start.

"Hello there."

They all looked up to see that the drawbridge had opened and walking toward them was a very strange-looking woman with pale skin and green hair and purple eyes. Cinders felt a big smile stretch across her face. This woman *had* to be magic. Maybe she would know something about her mom.

"Cinders, Hansel," the woman said with a deep curtsy. "And you must be Sparks and Mouse. I'm so happy you're here. I've been waiting for you. Won't you come inside?"

Chapter Fifteen

THERE'S SOMETHING OFF ABOUT *this*, thought Sparks as they followed the strange woman across the drawbridge and into the tower. Even though she smelled exactly like his favorite sausages, he could tell something was wrong, only he couldn't quite put his paw on what it was.

The moment they crossed into the Alabaster Tower, the heavy wooden draw-bridge shot upward, slamming shut behind them, and Sparks's fur began to prickle.

"Don't worry about that," the lady said. "We only have the drawbridge closed to keep others out."

Or to keep us in, Sparks thought to himself.

Even though Cinders hadn't seen any windows on the outside of the tower, the inside was filled with light. It was the very opposite of the Dark Forest, blindingly bright and beautiful—and, to Cinders, it smelled like freshly baked cookies and just-cut grass and the sparkling spring that ran through the bottom of her garden at home. It was the best smell she had ever smelled in all her smelling days.

"Now," said the woman, turning around to smile kindly at the questers. "Who's hungry?"

Mouse squeaked. He was very hungry, and the entire tower smelled deliciously of brie. It was so strong, he was rather tempted to give the walls a lick.

"I'm hungry!" Hansel held his hand up as high as he could. Whatever concerns he'd had about the tower before were far from his mind now. He could smell gingerbread and tree bark and a freshly washed pillowcase at the end of a long day, and he'd never been happier.

"That's good," said the lady, leading them farther into the tower, "because I've prepared a feast."

It was odd, thought Cinders. From the

outside the tower looked very skinny, but, now that they were inside, it seemed huge, with one room leading into another and then another and then another. She wasn't even sure if she could remember her way back to the drawbridge.

"Can anyone else hear crying?" asked Sparks, pricking up an ear. But no one could.

Cinders could hear the sound of hooves galloping and birds chirping. Hansel could hear the sound of his mother singing and the kettle boiling on the stove. Mouse couldn't tell them what he heard, but he could hear the sound of cheese being unwrapped. (Mouse had a fairly one-track mind.) Everyone could hear their absolute favorite thing in the world.

"Excuse me," Cinders said, her mouth

watering at the whiff of baked goods that hung heavy in the air, "but are you a fairy?"

"I'm a friend of the fairies," the woman replied. "They tell me things I need to know, and I help them when I can. You can call me Allaine."

"Did you say Alan?" Hansel muttered.

"It's a fairy thing," Cinders replied. "They're a bit weird about names. Don't worry about it."

"I don't get guests very often," said Allaine, ushering the four friends into another room and shutting the door behind them. "So I might have gone a little bit overboard with dinner. I do hope you'll find something here you like. I couldn't send you off to Fairyland on an empty stomach."

Cinders couldn't quite believe it. The

banquet at the palace had been impressive, and her magical breakfast with the three bears had been pretty great too, but never, ever in her life had she seen anything quite like this. In the middle of the room, piled high on a white crystal table, was the biggest mountain of food she had ever seen. Allaine had all her favorite things: brownies and muffins and Victoria sponge

and treacle cake and cookies and croissants and scones and chocolate torte and absolutely anything else you could think of. The other end of the table was laden with freshly baked gingerbread, jam sandwiches, tomato soup, and a piping hot blackberry pie, which just so happened to be Hansel's favorite thing in the whole world. And in the middle of it all were at least two dozen sausages and a whole wheel of cheese.

"Cinders," Sparks growled quietly. "I know this all looks delicious, but something isn't quite

right here. I don't think you should eat anything."

"Looks all right to me," Hansel said, pulling out a chair and sitting down at the table, trying to decide what to eat first.

Even though she desperately wanted to tuck into a particularly yummy-looking blueberry scone, Cinders had a teeny-tiny nagging feeling that Sparks might be right. And, when she listened extra hard, she was almost certain she *could* hear someone crying, as well.

"How did you know our names?" Cinders asked as she sat in the seat Allaine pulled out for her.

"The fairies told me," Allaine replied simply, still smiling.

"And how did you know all our favorite

foods?" Sparks asked, hiding underneath Cinders's legs.

"The fairies told me," Allaine repeated.

"Did they tell you who I am?" Cinders asked.

Allaine nodded. "You're Cinders. You live with your father and stepmother and stepsisters beyond the forest."

Cinders bit her lip. Time for the big question. "And what about my real mother?"

"Your real mother died when you were born," Allaine answered, "but I'm sure she would have been very proud of you."

"Did you know her?" Cinders asked.

"I've never met anyone from the human kingdom before," the woman replied, shaking her head. "The blobbles normally lead everyone away before they reach the tower."

So Allaine didn't seem to know Cinders's mom had been a fairy. That was very interesting.

"I think we should leave," Sparks said quietly, pulling on the leg of her trousers. "I've got a terrible feeling about this place."

If Sparks was prepared to walk away from a table full of sausages, something was definitely up. But everything looked so tasty and she was so hungry . . .

"Maybe just one bite," Cinders said, staring at a plump, fluffy scone positively bursting with raisins.

But Sparks wasn't having any of it. He jumped on the table in front of his friend and took a big sniff of all the food.

"Stop!" he barked loudly. "Do not eat a single bite! All this food has been cursed!"

"Say what?" Hansel said with a mouth full of pie.

"Oh, Hansel, no!" Cinders cried.

But it was too late.

Chapter Sixteen

BEFORE HANSEL COULD SPIT out the food, his eyes closed and his head plopped forward onto the table, face first into a big custard tart. Very, very loudly, he began to snore.

"Oh dear," Allaine said with an awkward laugh. "Perhaps my cooking skills aren't quite up to snuff. I'm sure the rest of it is okay. Do dig in."

"Not on your nelly!" shouted Cinders. "Get her, Sparks!"

And, with that, the shaggy red dog leaped off the table and went right for Allaine, who turned to run a moment too late. Before she could get anywhere, Sparks grabbed hold of the edge of her dress with his teeth and held his ground, growling loudly.

"Let go!" Allaine squealed as the fabric began to tear. "This is my best dress! My only dress!"

"Tell us what you're really doing here or

he'll be taking a bite out of your behind," Cinders ordered, even though they both knew Sparks had never, ever bitten anyone in his life.

"Fine!" the woman squeaked, her purple eyes flashing. "My job is to prevent anyone from the kingdom from finding their way to Fairyland, and to prevent anyone from Fairyland from finding their way to the kingdom. The fairies don't want anyone bothering them, especially not people who come from your kingdom, thank you very much."

"Well, that's not very nice, is it?" Cinders replied. "What's wrong with people from the kingdom?"

"I've heard lots of stories about you folk," Allaine sniffed. "You eat fairies, don't you?"

"We most certainly do not!" Cinders said

with great indignation. "What a terrible thing to say."

"That's what I heard and that's why the fairies don't want you in their land."

It was the most ridiculous thing Cinders had heard since Joderick had tried to convince her that fairies ate people. Why did everyone believe so much nonsense? Her dad always said, "Don't believe everything you hear!" and, good golly gosh, he was definitely right.

"Cinders?" Sparks said, his voice a bit muffled because his jaws were still firmly clamped down on the green-haired woman's skirt.

"Yes, Sparks?"

"What are we going to do now?"

Cinders planted her hands on her hips and stared at their would-be captor. Hmm. She hadn't thought that far ahead.

"I know," she said, suddenly excited. She turned to Allaine. "Take us to the person who's crying."

"Nope," Allaine said, shaking her head. "I'm afraid I can't do that."

Sparks growled and bit down a little harder.

"All right! This way—let's go, let's go!" Allaine squealed, leading them out of the banquet room and toward a tall spiral staircase.

Chapter Seventeen

"WELL, MUFFIN," JODERICK SAID, slowing his horse outside a particularly pretty-looking cottage in the middle of the Dark Forest, "this is where the map ends. Do you think Cinders is inside?"

The horse snuffled in response, still not altogether ecstatic about being dragged away from her warm, safe stables and ridden through a pitch-black forest all afternoon.

The prince's friend better be inside or Muffin was going to be well and truly miffed.

Joderick hopped off the horse's back and strode up the footpath, rubbing the toes of his riding boots on the back of his legs before he knocked on the door. The Dark Forest was a terribly grubby place. He couldn't help but think it might not be quite as dark if one of the royal gardeners got in there and did a spot of pruning from time to time. It wouldn't kill his father to lay a path while he was at it either.

After a moment or two, Joderick heard large, heavy footsteps inside the cottage that almost certainly didn't belong to Cinders. He took a deep breath and practiced his more regal facial expression, hoping that whoever was inside would be pleased to help a prince.

"We've had this place for five years and never has anyone so much as knocked at the door," a voice inside grumbled. "And now we've got people coming and going like we're a flipping hotel. I'm telling you, Karen, you never should have signed up for that mailing list."

"Be quiet and open the door," commanded another voice, "and tell them whatever they're selling, we don't want any."

The door creaked open to reveal a very tall, very furry, very angry-looking bear.

"Whatever it is, we don't want any," he growled.

"I'm not selling anything!" Joderick said in a voice that wasn't nearly as brave as he had hoped it might be. "It is I, Prince Joderick Jorenson Picklebottom, son of King Poderick Porenson Picklebottom the Fifth, and I am on a quest to help my friend Cinders, who I believe passed this way earlier today."

Before the big bear could say anything, Joderick heard the thunder of feet from inside the house and suddenly another pair of paws pushed the unwilling host out of the way.

"It *is* you!"

A second bear, shorter and wearing a very fetching floral dress, clasped her paws together in delight before clapping the prince on the shoulder and ushering him inside.

"Frank!" she yelled. "Get the kettle on! Don't you know who this is?"

"I'm not deaf," Frank muttered. "He just said he's the prince."

Of course, Joderick had no idea these were the very same bears Cinders had met that morning, otherwise he might have been a bit more understanding of Frank's bad mood. Eating all that magical breakfast had given him such a bellyache.

"Forgive my husband, sire," Karen said, all flustered by the presence of her royal visitor. "He doesn't keep up with the royal family like I do."

"No, I don't," Frank added. "Some of us are busy working for a living instead of reading all those gossip mags you've always got your nose in."

"You can call me Joderick," the prince said, smiling at a little cub who was lying on a rug in front of the television, playing with a mobile phone, and who didn't seem even slightly interested in the royal visitor. "Or Jodders. And there's no need to make tea—I really can't stay."

"You're looking for Cinders, you said?" Frank asked from the kitchen. "We sent her off toward the Alabaster Tower this morning."

"Alabaster Tower?" Joderick pulled out his map and looked for the landmark, but couldn't see it anywhere. "I've never heard of it before. Is that a new building?"

"Let me have a look at that," said Karen, spreading the map out neatly on her dining table. "No wonder you can't find it—you've only got half a map here."

Joderick screwed his face up in frustration. He must have ripped the map in two when he was escaping from his father's chambers! How was he going to find Cinders now?

"Never mind, never mind," she said, pulling bread and butter and a big block of cheese out of the cupboard. "We can give you the same directions we gave her. It's straight out of here and due north until you reach the tower. That's the halfway point to Fairyland."

"Thank you!" Joderick exclaimed, folding up his half map and preparing to leave. "Thank you so much."

"Ooh, must you dash off?" Karen asked, hands clasped against her heart. She'd longed to meet the prince. He'd always seemed so charming when she saw him interviewed on television, and here he was in the flesh, just as polite and twice as handsome. She couldn't wait to tell the girls in her book club all about it.

"Yes, you really should stay," grumbled Frank. "Have my bed, break the kid's chair, eat us out of house and home while you're at it."

"I'm afraid I have to go," Joderick said as Karen pulled him into a great big bear hug, "but I do appreciate your help."

"Anything for the royal family," she

replied, grabbing a piece of waxed paper out of the cupboard and hastily slapping together a sandwich cut with her claws. She couldn't possibly have him leaving empty-handed—whatever would the queen think?

"Um, thanks," said Joderick and turned to go.

As Mommy Bear and Daddy Bear were seeing the prince out, a very familiar face appeared on the television. The baby bear stared at the screen with his new puppy fast asleep at his feet. The king was explaining how his son, Prince Joderick, had gone missing and that there was a reward of a hundred gold pieces for his safe return. A hundred gold pieces would definitely pay for a new mobile, then he'd have a cool phone *and* a puppy!

Without stopping to think, he quickly tapped the number on the screen into his old phone and waited for someone to pick up.

"I just saw the prince in the Dark Forest and my mom made him a sandwich, but now he's gone," the baby bear declared. "Yes, I'll hold."

Hold for a hundred gold pieces, he thought, rubbing his paws together while his parents waved Prince Joderick off down the road.

Chapter Eighteen

HANSEL HAD BEEN RIGHT about one thing. There were a lot of stairs in the Alabaster Tower, and whoever was in charge of sweeping them definitely wasn't getting paid enough. Cinders was exhausted by the time they got to the top. Next time she saw Brian, she definitely had to ask about getting a pair of wings.

Allaine stood in front of a big black door with a very sulky look on her face.

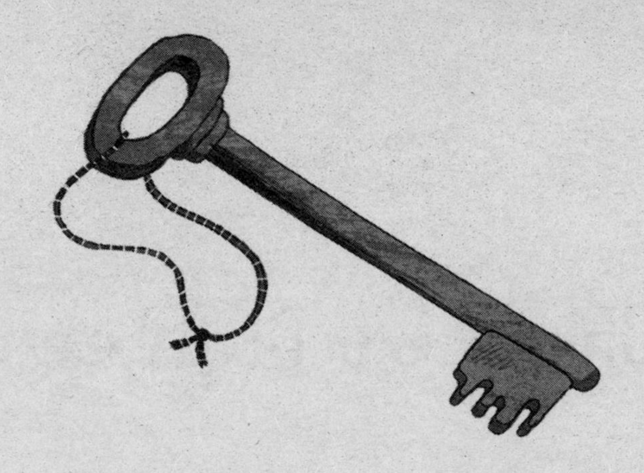

"Right, open it up," Cinders commanded, trying not to sound too out of breath.

"The fairies are going to be so mad," Allaine muttered as she produced a big black key from her pocket.

"They'll understand," Cinders replied. "I'll tell them I made you do it."

Allaine looked up at her and let out a surprised little laugh.

"I didn't mean they'd be mad with me,"

she cackled. "It's you who's going to be in trouble!"

Slowly, the door opened and inside was a tiny little room that seemed so much smaller on the inside than it did on the outside. The walls were white and smooth, like the rest of the tower, and at the very, very top, so high up Cinders couldn't even reach it if she stood on the tip of her tiptoes, was a tiny window. The floors were white, the ceiling was white, and right in the middle of the room was a bed, and right in the middle of the bed was a girl.

"Um, knock-knock," Cinders said, rapping her knuckles against thin air and stepping into the room. "Hope you don't mind visitors, only my friends and I heard you crying and I wanted to make sure you were okay."

The girl on the bed turned around and stared at Cinders as though she'd never seen another person before. She was very pretty, Cinders thought, with big brown eyes, clear, shining skin, and the longest hair Cinders had ever, ever seen. It flowed down her back, all the way to the floor before it disappeared under the bed. There were few things Cinders hated as much as washing and brushing her hair, and hers wasn't nearly as long as this girl's! It must have taken a full day just to braid it.

"I'm Cinders," she added when the girl didn't move. "What's your name?"

"Not the chatty type then," Sparks whispered as she continued to stare in silence. "I'm

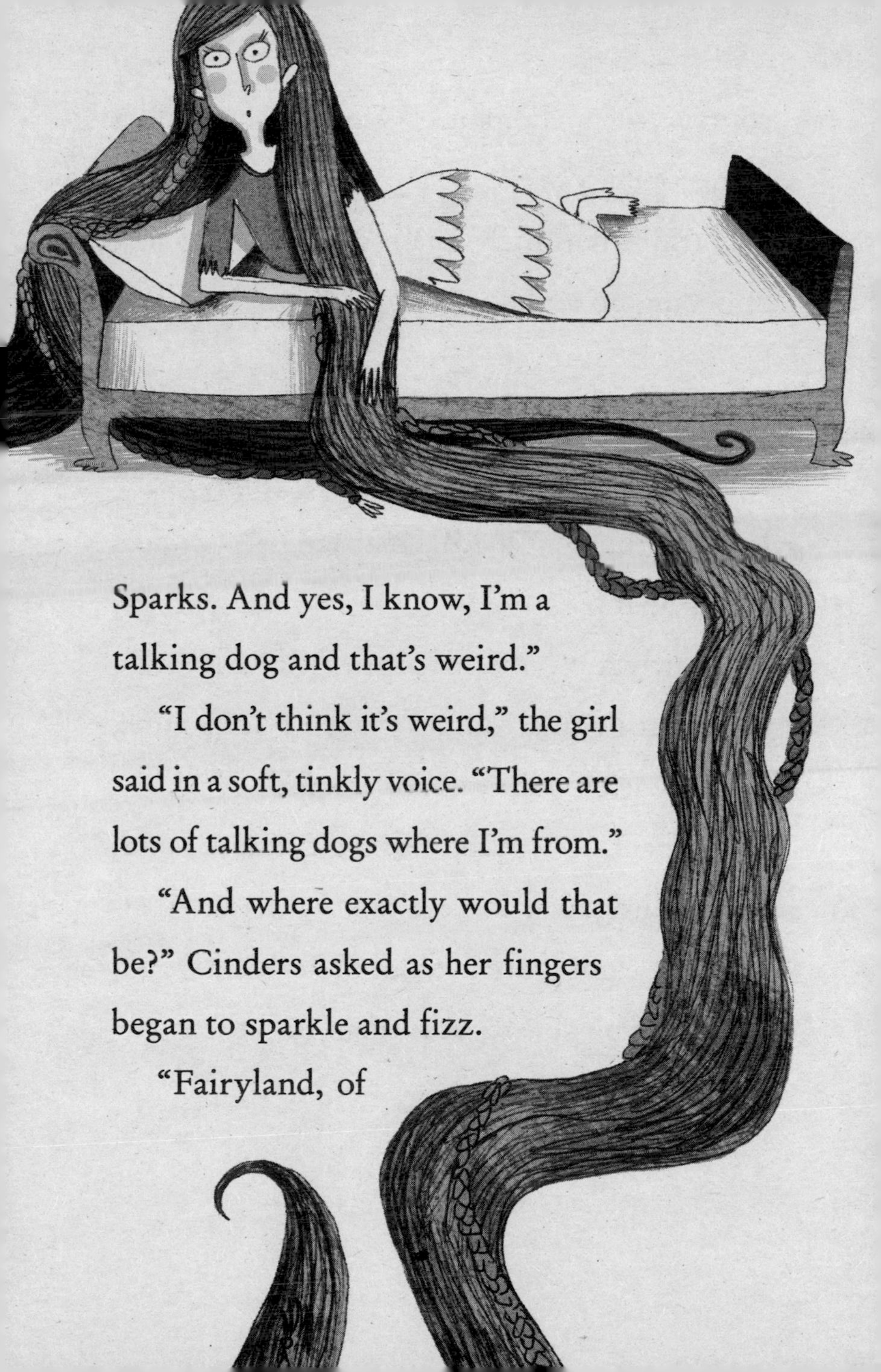

Sparks. And yes, I know, I'm a talking dog and that's weird."

"I don't think it's weird," the girl said in a soft, tinkly voice. "There are lots of talking dogs where I'm from."

"And where exactly would that be?" Cinders asked as her fingers began to sparkle and fizz.

"Fairyland, of

course," the girl replied. "Where else would a fairy come from?"

"You're definitely a fairy?" Cinders asked, bouncing up and down excitedly on the girl's bed.

"I am," she replied with a firm nod.

"Absolutely, positively, definitely one hundred percent a full, real fairy?" Cinders asked again.

"Fairly sure," the girl confirmed. "Although I've been in this room for such a long time, I've forgotten quite a lot of things."

"What's your name?" asked Cinders again, feeling altogether too excited. An actual, real-life fairy right there in front of her! She would definitely be able to help them find their way to Fairyland.

"It starts with an *R*," the girl said, concentrating so hard that a little sprinkle of pink glitter appeared over the top of her head. "Rappaport? Rapscallion?"

She's definitely a fairy, thought Sparks.

"Rapunzel!" The girl stood up with a happy start. "My name is Rapunzel!"

"Rapunzel," repeated Cinders slowly and carefully to make sure she got it exactly right. "How long have you been locked in this room?"

"When I first got here, I had a pixie cut," she replied and pulled her long, long braid out from underneath the bed. "Longer than you've been alive, I should think."

"This is all very nice," Allaine said, edging toward the door, "but why don't I run back downstairs and put the kettle on while you're all getting to know each other?"

"Why don't you stay exactly where you are," ordered Sparks, "and tell us why you've got Rapunzel locked up here in the first place?"

The green-haired woman gave a very loud huff. "It was for her own good. She was planning to run off to King Picklebottom's kingdom and get herself in all kinds of trouble. I was only trying to protect her. You do know those folks eat fairies?"

"For the last time, we most certainly do not," Cinders sighed, turning back to Rapunzel. "Why were you going to the kingdom?"

"I was looking for someone," she said with a faraway look. "My friend, I think."

"We're on our way to Fairyland to find out more about my mom!" Cinders exclaimed.

"Perhaps you could come with us and help us find our way."

"You're both talking nonsense," Allaine said, butting in before Rapunzel could answer. "You should both go back home and forget about all this silliness. No one cares who is or isn't missing from Fairyland anymore and, Cinders, have you even thought about how much trouble your father is in? Or Prince Joderick? You made the king very mad, and he's bound to take his temper out on someone!"

Cinders chewed nervously on her fingernail. She really hadn't thought about that. Poor Jodders. And her poor dad! He hadn't done anything wrong.

"Don't listen to her," Sparks said, giving

the woman a good growling. "She's trying to put you off your quest."

"You're right," replied Cinders, leaping to her feet and then sitting back down because she had a cramp in her left leg. "But what are we going to do with her when we leave?"

"You mustn't trust her," Rapunzel said. "She'll only cause trouble for you on your quest."

"Me?" Allaine gasped. "Cause trouble? *As if.*"

"There's only one thing we can do," Cinders said with a sigh, turning to Allaine. "I'm very sorry, but we're going to have to lock you up in this room."

"You can't do that!" Allaine protested. "That's a terrible thing to do!"

"You did it to Rapunzel! And don't

worry—we'll come back and let you out in a couple of days when we're done."

"If we feel like it," Sparks said, sticking his snout in the air.

Even though Cinders felt terrible about it, she and Rapunzel and Sparks walked out of the room at the top of the tower, leaving Allaine locked inside.

"Ooh, it's not so bad, is it?" Allaine called through the door. "This bed is actually very comfy. And I haven't had a nap in sixteen years. Don't rush back. I might have forty winks while you're gone."

"She's fine," Sparks said as Cinders popped the big black key in her pocket. "Both your father and Prince Joderick would want you to find Fairyland, which is exactly what we should be doing right now. What are we waiting for?"

"Yes," said Cinders. "You're right. Let's go."

From behind them, as they went down the stairs, came the sound of Allaine snoring.

Chapter Nineteen

GETTING DOWN THE STAIRCASE of the Alabaster Tower was much easier than getting up it. In no time at all, Cinders, Sparks, and Rapunzel were back in the banquet hall where Mouse waited patiently and Hansel remained fast asleep.

"The best way to wake someone from an enchanted sleep is with a kiss," Rapunzel whispered as Cinders tried to pry her friend's eyelids open.

"No, I don't think so," she replied, poking him in the ribs, pinching his arm, and punching his funny bone.

"It is traditional," Rapunzel said, shrugging her shoulders. "And it's a great way to get a snog from a prince."

"Look, I'm not going to kiss him," Cinders said, hands on hips. "I've never kissed him before, he hasn't asked me to kiss him, I don't want to kiss him, and you don't go around kissing people while they're asleep! It's very rude. Also, he isn't a prince—he's just Hansel."

"He's very handsome," Rapunzel said as she popped his hat back on his head. It had fallen off into a big pile of mini muffins.

"Is he?" Cinders looked at his upturned nose and chestnut hair and ruddy cheeks, but she couldn't see it. Jodders was definitely handsome, everyone said so, but Hansel? Rapunzel had been locked up in that room for too long.

"Oh for goodness' sake!" Sparks leaped up on the table and gave Hansel a big, sloppy slurp, right on the lips, and right away, his eyes began to flicker open.

"There we are," Cinders said, very relieved. Handsome or not, she had not wanted to explain this situation to his mother or Gretel. "Now no one needs to kiss anyone."

"Why does my face smell like sausages?" Hansel mumbled, rubbing his eyes. "How long was I asleep?"

"Not long enough," Cinders said, patting her horse's back. "Are you ready to go, Mouse?"

Mouse squeaked happily at his friend and twitched his pink ears.

"Oh, that's very funny," Rapunzel laughed as they made their way outside. "You're such a comedian, Mouse."

"You can understand him?" Cinders asked, her eyes wide.

She nodded as though it was a fact that should have been very obvious to everyone. "All fairies can talk to animals," she explained. "And fairy princesses can even talk to trees and plants."

"Then it would have been very useful to

have a fairy princess when we were traveling through the Dark Forest," Cinders said. "You don't know where we can find one, do you?"

"Oh!" Rapunzel clapped her hands to her face. "That's it!"

"What's it?" Hansel asked, peeking at the fairy's back as a large, colorful pair of wings appeared out of nowhere. They were very delicate, almost see-through, but, when the light hit them, the wings shimmered with every color of the rainbow.

"The fairy princess!" Rapunzel exclaimed, fluttering her wings with excitement. "That's who I was looking for! When she went missing, all of Fairyland was so sad. I was sure if I could find her and bring her back, everyone would be happy again."

"Do you think she's lost in the forest?"

Cinders said, a little worried. Fairies might be magical, but they weren't always blessed with much common sense, and the Dark Forest was a dangerous place to be. She could easily imagine someone getting lost in there for years and years.

"I hope not, but wherever she is I'll find her," Rapunzel promised. "Just as I hope you find your way safely to Fairyland!"

And, with that, a stream of pink sparkles

shot from her hands and the big wooden drawbridge opened with a thud. Before Cinders could say another word, the fairy was flying away.

"Wait!" she cried. "How do we get to Fairyland from here?"

"It's not far," Rapunzel called back. "Simply traverse the Empty Valley and travel along the mountain pass and then you're there! Shouldn't take more than a few weeks."

And, with a puff of pink smoke, she vanished.

"A few weeks!" Cinders collapsed on the ground and crossed her legs. "I didn't think it was going to take nearly that long."

"Neither did I," sighed Sparks, scratching

his ear with his hind leg. "This is not good news at all."

"Say, Cinders." Hansel pulled a mini muffin out of his hat. "How long did that fairy say she'd been trapped in this tower?"

"She wasn't sure," Cinders replied sadly, "but she thought it was probably longer than I'd been alive. Why?"

"Just thinking," he said as he shook crumbs out of his hair. "You don't reckon the fairy

princess she's looking for could be your mom, do you?"

Cinders stared at her friend with wide eyes.

"Because if she is," he went on, completely oblivious to the shock on his friend's face, "that would make you a princess too! How cool would that be?"

"Good golly gosh," Cinders whispered, looking up into the clear blue sky. What an idea.

"I really think we should get going," Sparks said, ever the voice of reason. "It certainly isn't getting any earlier and Fairyland isn't getting any closer."

"You got it, Sparks." Hansel grabbed Mouse's rein and directed him, clip-clopping, over the drawbridge. "Anyway, it's just a thought, Cinders."

"Just a thought," she agreed, her mind wandering as she followed her friends. "I'm sure it's not the case. I mean, if I was a fairy princess, even half a one, surely I'd be better at magic." And have neater hair. And princesses hardly ever had to do the dishes. Cinders did the washing-up all the time.

But, she thought as Bloop the blobble reappeared and waved them on their way, *but, but, but . . . What if Hansel was right?*

What if her mom was the missing fairy princess?

What if she was a fairy princess too?

Chapter Twenty

THE CREATURES OF THE Dark Forest didn't usually get a lot of visitors, but on this particular day, the dank, dismal woodland was busier than a very busy place indeed. First Cinders, Hansel, Sparks, and Mouse had traveled along its tracks, followed by brave Prince Joderick Jorenson Picklebottom, and now, as the sun began to set, one more citizen from the kingdom rode his horse into the forest.

The Huntsman.

A little way back from the dense line of trees, at a safe distance from any stray nobble-dizooks who might be passing by, Margery, Elly, Aggy, and the royal family watched him disappear into the darkness on his tall black horse.

"Do you think he'll find my beloved prince?" asked Elly, more hopeful than she was afraid.

"Let's hope so," Margery sniffed.

"Do you think he'll find Cinders?" asked Aggy, more afraid than she was hopeful.

"Let's hope not," Margery muttered.

"The Huntsman has never failed on a mission," King Picklebottom said, tucking his thumbs into his belt. It was new and the buckle was very shiny and he really wanted everyone to see it. "Well, except for that one time . . ."

"He'll have both of them back home before sunset tomorrow," the queen confirmed. "Right where they belong. Joderick in the palace, and Cinders in the dungeon."

As the black horse rode farther into the forest, the sounds of the royal family faded away. The deadly nightshade closed up its petals and even the munklepoops ran to hide as the Huntsman rode by. No one wanted to be on the wrong side of him and, even though she didn't know it, that was exactly where Cinders was at that very moment.

His horse seemed to fly through the woods, the trees bending and bowing to make room, and the darkness didn't bother him at all. He could see perfectly well without the sun. As he rode onward, not far from the three bears' cottage, a certain fairy godmother popped into the forest with a fizz and a crackle and a sprinkling of silver sparkles.

"Cinders?" Brian called out. "Did you call?"

Of course Cinders had called, except it had been several hours earlier, and now she was many, many miles away. Fairy communications were far from reliable. Much better to send a text or something, but, for the life of her, Brian couldn't work out mobile phones. Too many buttons, not enough magic and, for some reason, hers was always tweeting. She once took it apart, looking for a little bird inside, but she couldn't find anything but wires and the like.

"Cinders! Where are you?"

The fairy was investigating a suspicious blue spot on her pale pink skirt when she

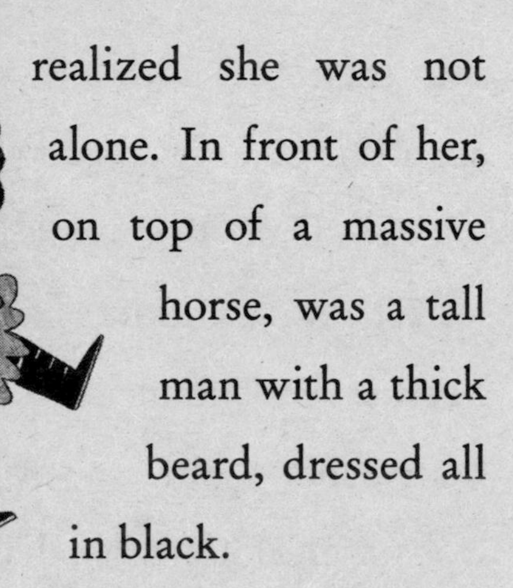

realized she was not alone. In front of her, on top of a massive horse, was a tall man with a thick beard, dressed all in black.

"You're not Cinders," she said simply.

The Huntsman grabbed his horse's reins and pulled them sharply, making the horse rear up on its back legs (which it really didn't enjoy at all).

"Where is the girl?" he barked.

Brian eyed him warily. This was why she preferred not to leave Fairyland. You never knew when you were going to run into complete twonks like this.

"I'm sorry, have we met?" she asked politely.

"Tell me where she is or I'll chop off your head," the Huntsman roared, brandishing a rather impressive sword. If you were into that kind of thing.

"You, sir, are very rude," Brian replied.

It was a shame, really, she thought to herself. If he shaved off the beard or at least trimmed it a bit, he'd be quite a good-looking chap. She might have invited

him to tea if he hadn't been trying to hunt down her fairy goddaughter.

"I will find her with or without your help," the Huntsman said, giving Brian quite the look before spurring his horse on and disappearing into the darkness.

"Oh, I say," Brian muttered. "What a drama queen. All talk and no trousers, that one. I can tell."

And, even though she was pretty sure she could take him if it came down to a fight, she waved her wings and disappeared.

Better to find Cinders before the Huntsman did, just in case . . .

The End (for now . . .)

TURN THE PAGE FOR A SNEAK PEEK AT THE NEXT BOOK IN THE SERIES!

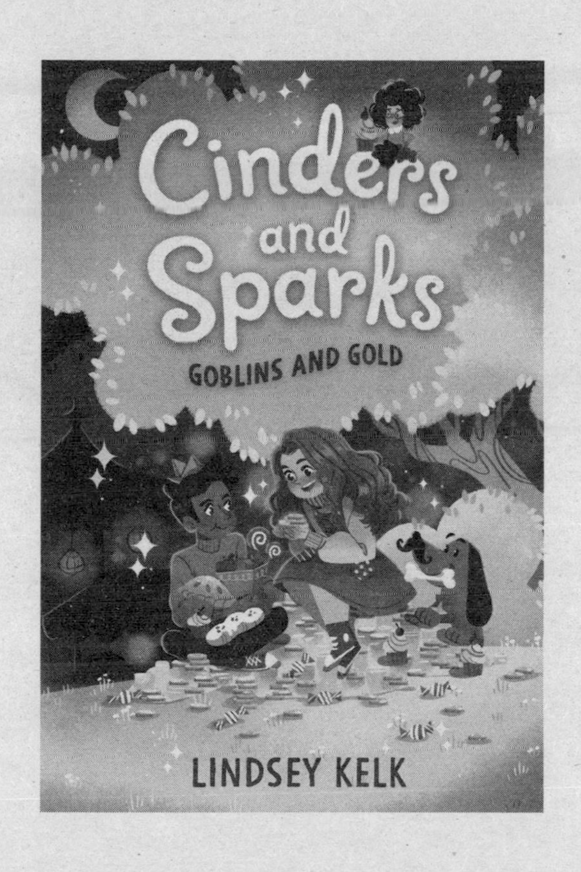

Chapter One

CINDERS WAS A GIRL with a lot on her mind. Here she was, trotting through a forest on a horse that used to be a mouse, with her best friend, who just so happened to be a talking dog, and a boy in a green hat named Hansel. But she wasn't thinking about any of them. She was thinking about her mom, her dad, and a little bit about where they were going to get their lunch.

"You're very quiet," Hansel said from the back of Mouse the horse.

"Am I?" Cinders replied.

"I don't like it when you're quiet," Hansel said. "It's weird."

"Don't get used to it," Sparks piped up from his spot in front of Cinders, his head nestled in Mouse's mane. "I think this is the longest she's gone without speaking since she learned to talk."

"What if Hansel is right?" Cinders began. "What if my mom was the princess who went missing from Fairyland all those years ago?"

Sparks sighed. *There goes my peace and quiet*, he thought to himself.

The four friends were on a quest. Cinders had recently found that she could do magic and it turned out it was because her mother had been a fairy. Unfortunately, she couldn't ask her mother about that because she had died soon after Cinders was born, and she couldn't ask her father because he was back at home in the kingdom. The kingdom was the one place Cinders definitely could not return to because the king hated magic and would throw her in the dungeons for sure. Mostly because of an accidental wish-granting incident that saw

King Picklebottom bitten on the bottom by a roast pig Cinders had not-at-all-on-purpose brought back to life.

The king hated magic, which meant the king hated Cinders. It was all quite a mess.

"It was just an idea," Hansel said,

scratching his hair underneath his hat. "Although I am very often right about things."

(He wasn't.)

Hansel had joined the quest after helping himself to one too many delicious tiles from the roof of his neighbor's gingerbread house. Mouse had joined the quest after Cinders turned him into a horse and he found he quite liked it. Sparks had joined the quest because Cinders was his best friend and, even if she was quite loud, occasionally annoying, and never packed enough sausages, he loved her more than anything.

"Besides," Hansel said, "surely you'd know if your mom was a fairy princess. Wouldn't you have extra-extra-special powers or something?"

"You mean something like magical, sparkly fingers that make wishes come true?" Cinders suggested. "And let's not forget that time I flew."

"I'm not sure floating fifteen centimeters off the ground counts as flying," Sparks said with a gruffly yawn. "I've got an idea—why don't you wish up some lunch? I'm getting hungry."

That was hardly a surprise. Sparks was almost always starving.

"I don't think I'll have to," Cinders said. She gave the air a big sniff. "Can you smell that?"

"Freshly baked bread!" Hansel gasped. His mouth began to water. "Oh, what I wouldn't give for a nice slice of toast."

"Come on, Mouse, let's go and find something to eat." Cinders flicked the reins and Mouse picked up speed, galloping through the forest, following the delicious aromas that wafted toward them.

For the first time in ages, the twisted tree trunks of the Dark Forest parted and Cinders could see the blue sky overhead. And not just the sky, but beyond the line of the forest she saw a towering mountain in the distance, fields full of pink grass, and colorful houses dotted along a blue-bricked road. At the end of the road was a market.

"I don't want to exaggerate," Sparks said, sitting up in Cinders's lap, "but this might be the most excited I have ever been. Markets almost always mean sausages."

"Agreed," said Cinders as they clip-clopped onto the blue bricks. "Let's go and find some snacks!"

In no time at all, they arrived at the market.

Even though it looked like any other market from a distance, close up Cinders could tell it was somehow different. The stalls were brightly colored, gleaming cascades

of silk covered
the tables and stands, and the
air was filled with the sweetest
smells. The market stalls
in the kingdom all

used rough canvas or white cotton to cover their stands and, no matter what day of the week it was, all Cinders could ever smell was fish, and Cinders hated the smell of fish.

Neither Sparks nor Hansel were able to do magic themselves, but, if they could have granted a wish or two, they would have magicked something very much like the food they found at the very first market stall. Big, plump, juicy sausages for Sparks, freshly baked cakes for Cinders, and, well, Hansel wasn't fussy. He would happily eat anything.

"Everything looks delicious," Cinders said, her mouth watering.

"It does," Hansel agreed, looking around the marketplace. "But are we sure it's safe to eat? I don't think these people are quite like us."

Cinders looked up from a particularly appealing sweet stall that sold seventeen different flavors of fudge.

"What do you mean?" she asked.

"Look," Hansel whispered, nodding at a man walking by. "They're weird."

The person in question was much shorter than Cinders or Hansel and his skin was a very pale purple color. His spiky hair was bright green and his big, smiling eyes were such a bold yellow that Cinders was certain she'd be able to see them in the dark.

"They just look different than us, that's all," Cinders said, her own eyes again fixed firmly on the fudge. "Not everyone's the same."

"I suppose so," Hansel replied. She had a point. Up until a couple days ago, he'd never met a dog that could talk, but Sparks wasn't weird. A bit rude sometimes, but that was just Sparks.

"Excuse me," Cinders said to the blue-haired lady behind the fudge counter.

She turned and gasped, looking Cinders up and down in surprise.

Hmm, Cinders thought, *Hansel isn't the only one who thinks certain people here look odd. They're as confused by us as we are by them!*

"How much is your vanilla-strawberry-chocolate-chip fudge?"

"All the fudge is one gold piece per bag," the lady replied, eyeing the group curiously. It wasn't often they saw people from the kingdom beyond the Dark Forest. In fact, she had only ever met one person from there before in her entire life and she hoped never to run into him again. She shivered, thinking of his big black hood and big black boots.

"Thank you very much," Cinders said with a huge smile before turning back to her friends. "Okay, the fudge is one gold piece per bag. Hansel, how much money have you got with you?"

"Absolutely none," he replied.

"And I've got—" Cinders dug her hands deep into her pockets—"a button. Flipping fiddlesticks! How are we going to buy something to eat if we don't have the money to pay for it?"

"Um, Cinders," Sparks said, pointing to a poster with his front paw. "I think we might have a bigger problem right now."

Cinders gasped.

Nailed to the tree behind her was a wanted poster.

A wanted poster with her picture on it!

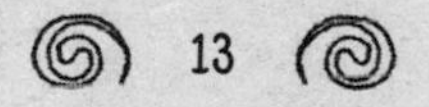

WANTED

Chapter Two

EVEN THE BRAVEST PRINCE in the entire world might have been a little bit nervous riding through the Dark Forest on his own, and Prince Joderick Jorenson Picklebottom was the first to admit he was hardly the bravest prince in the entire world. Joderick was the kind of prince who would much rather spend his days baking a perfect chocolate soufflé or playing video games. But here he was, riding his horse, Muffin, through the darkest part of the Deep Dark Very Incredibly Scary Forest, looking for his friend Cinders.

"So . . . which way do you think we should go?" Joderick asked Muffin as they came to a fork in the trail.

Muffin snorted in response. She wasn't magic like Sparks, so she couldn't tell him what she thought. And, if she could, she didn't think he would appreciate her response very much anyway.

Joderick looked down at the map he had secretly borrowed without asking from his father's private desk, and frowned at the big tear that ran right down the edge. Joderick must have ripped it when he pulled it out of the desk, and now he had reached the end of the trail marked on the parchment. He had no idea where to go next.

"Why is it, whenever I bump into people from the kingdom, they're always hanging around like spare parts?"

Joderick looked up from his map to see a woman standing right in front of him. He blinked and rubbed his eyes. Where had she come from? She wasn't there a minute ago. And he couldn't help but notice that her hair was very red and her skin was very pale and, if he wasn't much mistaken, she had a pair of quite impressive wings sprouting out of the middle of her back.

"Giddy gumdrops," Joderick whispered. "You're a fairy."

"I'm not getting anything past you, am I?" she replied. "What's wrong with you? Never seen a fairy before?"

"A-actually, n-no," he said, stuttering over every word. "Fairies are banned from the kingdom. Are you going to eat me?"

That did it. The fairy started laughing as though Joderick had said the funniest thing she'd ever heard. She laughed so hard, she fell to the ground with a hard **PLOP!**, tears streaming from her eyes and fogging up her glasses. (Yes, some fairies do need glasses. Just because they can grant wishes

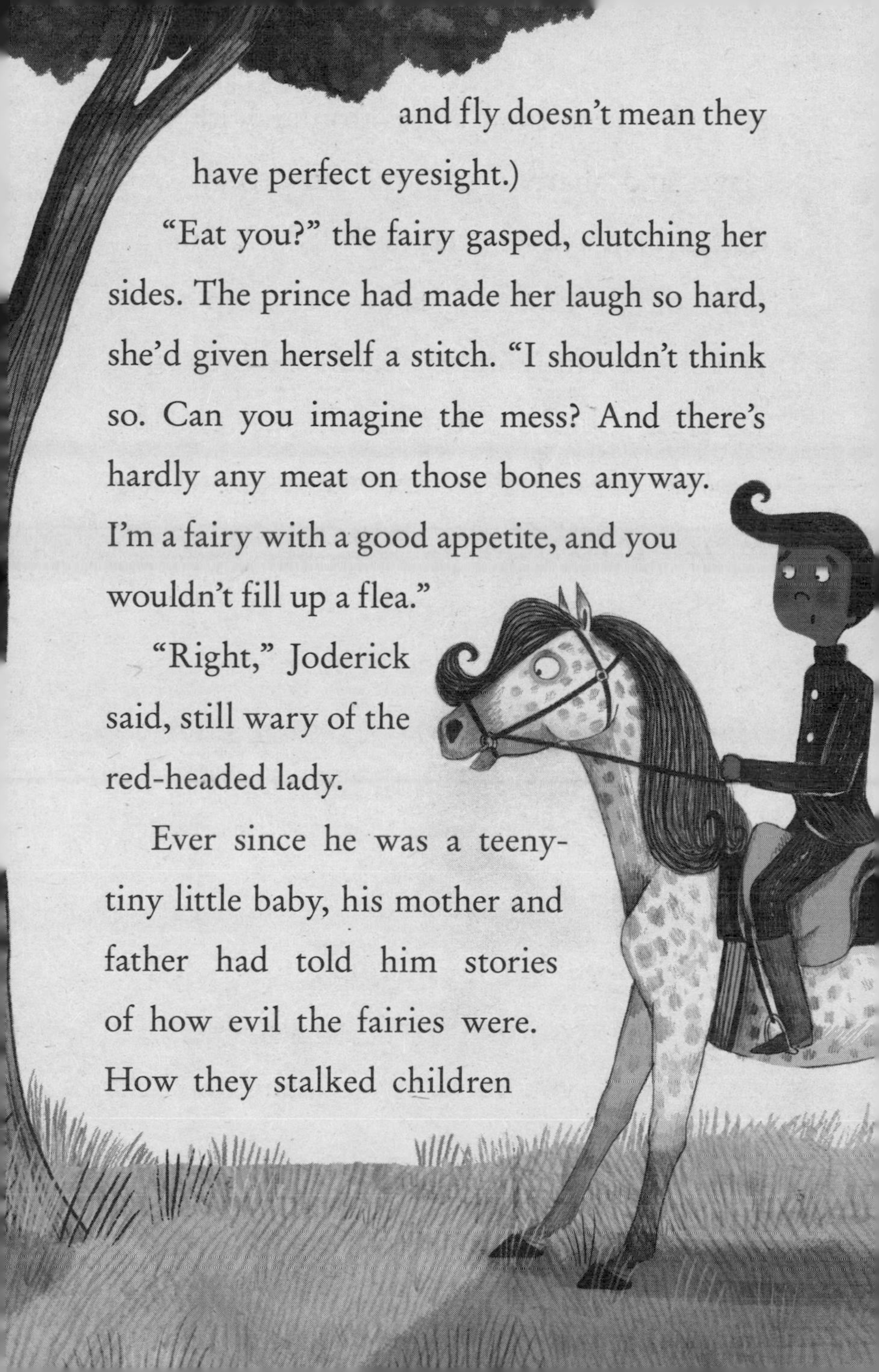

and fly doesn't mean they have perfect eyesight.)

"Eat you?" the fairy gasped, clutching her sides. The prince had made her laugh so hard, she'd given herself a stitch. "I shouldn't think so. Can you imagine the mess? And there's hardly any meat on those bones anyway. I'm a fairy with a good appetite, and you wouldn't fill up a flea."

"Right," Joderick said, still wary of the red-headed lady.

Ever since he was a teeny-tiny little baby, his mother and father had told him stories of how evil the fairies were. How they stalked children at night, how they crept around with long claws and sharp teeth, and how they were determined to take over the kingdom. But this fairy didn't have long claws or sharp teeth, and she certainly didn't seem very interested in eating him. In fact, she'd already pulled a cupcake out of her bag and was happily tucking into that instead.

"I'm looking for a girl," the fairy said, a dollop of icing on the end of her nose. "About your height, fair hair, very messy, probably covered in muck and with food all over her face."

Joderick's eyes widened.

"You wouldn't be talking about Cinders by any chance, would you?" he asked.

"How do you know my goddaughter?" the fairy replied.

"She's my friend. I'm looking for her too," Joderick said, completely gobsmacked. "You're Cinders's godmother?"

"Yes."

"But you're a fairy!"

"Sharpest knife in the drawer, aren't you, clever clogs?" Brian muttered to herself. "Yes, I'm Cinders's godmother and yes, I'm a fairy and, as I mentioned, I'm looking for her. Have you seen her or not because I'm in something of a rush. There's a very large man with a very large ax roaming around these woods who is also looking for her and I'd much prefer it if I found her first."

All the color drained from Joderick's face.

"I really, really, really, really hope you aren't talking about the Huntsman," he said, holding Muffin's reins a little bit tighter.

"That's him," Brian said with a chuckle. "Fancies himself a bit, doesn't he?"

Joderick was very pleased to be up on his horse because he was shaking so much that if he'd been down on the ground, Brian would have seen his knees knocking together.

"The Huntsman is the most feared man in the entire kingdom," he said in a wobbly voice. "He has never failed to complete a mission. Whatever he hunts, he catches. He isn't scared of anything."

Brian shrugged. "Everyone is scared of something. For me, it's guinea pigs. I don't like their little hands . . ."

"I'm serious!" Joderick told her, trying not to sound too wibbly. "Anything you tell him to find, he finds it. And I don't think he always asks nicely."

He knew his father would say it wasn't very becoming for a prince to sound so scared, but they were talking about the Huntsman, and he was after Cinders.

"I don't know what you're so worried about," Brian said, fluttering her wings until she was up on her feet once again. "Like I said, everyone is afraid of something, and I happen to have an inkling of what will scare him."

"What are you, some sort of mind reader?" Joderick asked.

"Yes," she replied confidently.

Joderick wasn't sure if she was being serious or not, but she very much looked like she was.

"The bigger they come, the harder they fall," Brian went on. "Besides, all we have to do is find Cinders first and then we needn't worry about him."

"And how are we going to do that?" Joderick asked.

She looked at him with a little smile on her shining face.

"Magic," she said, snapping her fingers.

And, just like that, they both

disappeared.